Praise

"As graceful and cor
ing."

—NPR Books

"Wise readers will hop on this train now, as the journey promises to be breathtaking."

—Robin Hobb, author of *The Assassin's Apprentice*

"This is an impressive performance."

—*Publishers Weekly*

"I am impressed... An exceedingly inventive story in a lushly realized dark setting that is not your uncle's Medieval Europe. I'll be looking forward to the next installment."

—Glen Cook, author of *The Black Company*

"Bradley P. Beaulieu's new fantasy epic is filled with memorable characters, enticing mysteries, and a world so rich in sensory detail that you can feel the desert breeze in your hair as you read. Çeda is hands-down one of the best heroines in the genre—strong, resourceful, and fiercely loyal to friends and family. Fantasy doesn't get better than this!"

—C. S. Friedman, author of the Coldfire and Magister trilogies

"Exotic, sumptuous and incredibly entertaining, Beaulieu has created memorable characters in a richly imagined world."

—Michael J. Sullivan, author of *The Riyria Chronicles*

"Beaulieu's intricate world-building and complex characters are quickly becoming the hallmarks of his writing, and if this opening volume is any indication, The Song of the Shattered Sands promises to be one of the next great fantasy epics."

—Jim Kellen, Science Fiction and Fantasy Book Buyer for Barnes & Noble

"Beaulieu's fantasy worlds are well-imagined and richly drawn...the kind you want to keep visiting."

—Kirkus Speculative Reading List for September 2015

Also by Bradley P. Beaulieu

The Song of the Shattered Sands
Of Sand and Malice Made
Twelve Kings in Sharakhai
With Blood Upon the Sand
A Veil of Spears

Shattered Sands Novellas
The Doors at Dusk and Dawn
In the Village Where Brightwine Flows
The Tattered Prince and the Demon Veiled
A Wasteland of My God's Own Making

The Lays of Anuskaya
The Winds of Khalakovo
The Straits of Galahesh
The Flames of Shadam Khoreh

Short Story Collections
Lest Our Passage Be Forgotten & Other Stories
In the Stars I'll Find You & Other Tales of Futures Fantastic

Novellas
The Burning Light (with Rob Zeigler)
Strata (with Stephen Gaskell)

The Tattered Prince and the Demon Veiled

BRADLEY BEAULIEU

First Edition: November 2017

ISBN: 978-1-93964-929-4 (Paperback)
ISBN: 978-1-93964-927-0 (epub)
ISBN: 978-1-93964-928-7 (Kindle)

Please visit me on the web at
http://www.quillings.com

The Tattered Prince and the Demon Veiled

In the western quarter of the Amber City lies a congested riddle of streets known as the Knot. There, a man named Brama walks, cloaked in the anonymity awarded to men who keep their heads down and their words to themselves. Years ago Brama would have refused to walk these streets, not without due compensation, in any case, and he certainly wouldn't have called them home. He'd been a street tough then, a rangy gutter wren with the skill of a locksmith and the heart of a thief. He'd been brash, even bold, but no one would have called him brave. He would have laughed at the very thought of the Knot becoming familiar to him, but the wheel turns and times change. Brama is no longer the same man he was then. The young Brama wouldn't even recognize him.

Truth be told, Brama could live in any quarter of the city he chose, but he calls this hellish place home for one simple reason: the Knot is populated by those who've learned to keep to themselves. To be sure, there are wolves as well as sheep. They prowl, preying on the weak, but Brama was never much of a victim, and only a fool would call him one now. If the pattern of scars over his face, neck, and arms aren't enough to convince, his black-laugher scowl certainly is.

For his part, Brama doesn't much care what anyone thinks of him as long as they leave him in peace. He exists, whiling away the days, nursing his dwindling fortune, wondering what the city and the desert gods have in store for him. He's been in the Knot for nearly two years—me along with him—and he's begun to wonder if the gods have forgotten him.

Surely the gods would not have forgotten a man like Brama, though they may have grown bored of his indolence, which would explain why, on this particular day, instead of heading toward his room above the tannery, Brama breaks his routine and heads down a back alley for the banks of the Haddah. Spring rains have returned to the desert, and the river is swelling.

He goes to the place he favored when he was young and watches a group of children playing skipjack. One by one they sprint and leap from the bank onto a canvas held taut by their gleeful friends, bounce into the air, arms and legs flailing, and fall into the surging water below. Some of them he still recognizes, though they've clearly grown; others are new. Their laughs and their games make him feel as though he's passed beyond the veil and now watches the world of the living, his feet forever rooted in the further fields. That's what his father used to say happened to those who pine for their old lives. And he does pine at times, so much that it hurts.

Sitting in the shade of the embankment, hidden beneath his cowl, he watches those gutter wrens the whole afternoon. He stands only when the children exit the water, still dripping, ready to depart en masse. How he wishes he could join them. How he wishes he could run the streets as he once did. But that was a different life. And he is now a different man.

As he turns to leave, he spots a girl watching the same group of children, pining, perhaps, as Brama was, for younger, simpler days. The girl is young yet herself. If she's seen more than fifteen summers, I'm an innocent lamb set for slaughter. Red ribbons are braided through her hair, a common style in the city of late, and she wears the simple clothes of a lowborn Sharakhani girl, but there's something odd about her. She stands tall, clasping her hands before her as a poet might before reading her lines. It's unconscious, I'm certain, a tell as plain as one could be.

Perhaps aware of being watched, she turns and takes note of Brama, scans the riverbank and the plaza behind him with chary eyes, then rushes away. Even in this she has the posture and bearing of a noblewoman. But this isn't the most interesting thing about her—to Brama *or* to me. It is the fact that, since the moment he spotted her, there were notes of light surrounding her. Like sundogs shining in a cloud-scraped sky, they shimmer, they glimmer. They brighten here and dim there. They move with her like the desert wind summoning demons from the sand as it gusts through Sharakhai's tight and winding streets.

She glances back several times, but Brama chooses not to follow. He can see she's scared, and who can blame her? The way Brama looks she'd be a fool not to be a *little* scared. Then she's gone, lost down an alley. There's a strange yearning that follows her absence. A deep desire for…something. Her presence? *Foolish*, Brama thinks. He doesn't even know her. But then he wonders…

From around his neck he removes a leather necklace. Strung there like an amulet is a falcon's egg sapphire. It's one of the more priceless gems in all the desert, but one would never know by looking at it, with its surfaces grimed with oil and soot. It's wrapped tightly in leather cord so that it looks like a cargo net lifting a dirty chunk of sky. This is my prison, the place I've been held since Brama and the girl known as the White Wolf trapped me here.

Wrapping the leather necklace around his hand with a flick of his wrist, Brama tightens his grip on the gemstone and steps down into the mud. His sandals sink as he walks, squelch as he trudges forward. When he comes to a place where the water has pooled, he squats and stares into a reflection that is imperfect— much like the landscape of his scar-torn face. The scars are an unsubtle reminder of a time when *I* was the master and *he* the chained. He was a comely man once—even *I* recognize that, a being who'd seen countless years pass in the Shangazi. It might have been why I was so pleased to make him cut himself; something about seeing himself destroy his own beauty pleased me. Part of me now regrets having done it to him, but I was wroth with the godling children who'd come for me; wroth as well that I'd been forced to take Brama when the one I'd really wanted was the White Wolf.

"She was never yours to take," Brama said to his reflection.

For months now Brama has somehow been able to hear snippets of my thoughts. It happens when my guard is down, so of course I quickly replace my walls, but I know already they will fail once more—my will is strong, as is my god-given power, but nothing I have done in this place seems to last.

In the water's reflection, a new visage forms, slowly replacing his. Long black spikes lift from his scalp as his curly locks of hair recede. Horns jut from a black-skinned forehead, curving back and around like a ram's crown carved from ebony. Slanted eyes tinged with rust replace the green of Brama's, and while Brama had always possessed features that were fair, more feminine cheeks and lips and chin replace his own.

Fear, as it always does, builds in Brama breast. It isn't so much as it once was, though, which pleases me greatly. He of all people knows the danger I represent, but he's become accustomed to me, a necessary first step in gaining my freedom and all the *more* important considering the effect we just witnessed illuminating that girl.

I say to him, "What is it you wish, my master?"

"How many times must I ask you not to call me that?"

"Are you not my master?"

"You are a fiend, and my enemy."

My visage laughs, and both of us feel a brightening, a candle lit and doused in as little time as it takes a mortal child to giggle. "What shall I call you, then? Brama the Mighty? Brama the Bold?"

Though he chooses not to reply, curiosity overrides his fears, creating a strange alchemy of caution and hope. "Tell me of the girl," he says. "Why was she twinkling like that?"

"It's how I see you sometimes."

"Mortals, you mean."

"Yes."

"But why does it happen? What has it revealed about her?"

"It means that she is someone who will affect your fate, or the fate of others who are dear to you, or both. It means she is someone around whom the winds of fate do whorl."

"That tells me nothing."

"It's no more complex than predicting the weather by judging the clouds and the smell in the air. It is another form of sight, granted me by Goezhen, or perhaps a thing passed to me when I was crafted from his soul. Who can know any longer?"

"Is that why you wanted Çeda? Was *she* like that?"

"Oh, yes." How bright that one had been. How very bright.

Brama considers this for a time, and I wonder what happened by the river. He'd been as transfixed as I, watching that girl rush away from the Haddah. For the first time since I've known him, I feel curiosity emanating from him like heat from a brand, and an urge to involve himself in something, anything, outside the tiny world he's made for himself. I resist the instinct to influence him—he's grown disturbingly good at sensing when I'm doing so. Instead, I simply wait.

"Shall I find her again?" he finally asks.

I hide my grin as I speak, "That is completely up to you, my Lord Brama."

He seems irked by the answer but says nothing in return. Slowly, my visage fades from the silty puddle, until he's staring at himself once more. He runs his fingers over the kindling-pile pattern of his scars. He stares around, to the now-empty banks of the Haddah. He feels the empty space inside him opening up again. He may hide it from others but I know how desperate he's been to find someone. A friend with whom he can share stories. A woman he might love and be loved by. He's confusing the lights with the sort of young love all mortal youths seem to experience. I do nothing to disabuse him of the notion—it is yet another step on the long road to freedom, after all—but it also touches my heart. I've not lived with humanity for so long that I am unaffected by the emotions my hosts feel.

Soon, he's standing and tugging on the cowl that keeps his face hidden from the world. His mind is elsewhere at last, and it leaves me alone with my secret. The girl. The lights around her. It's true that they are tied to Brama's fate. But more accurately, they are tied to mine, and I have no doubt now that this girl will be the key to escaping my faceted prison once and for all.

Three days pass before Brama spots the same girl. He's standing in a darkened doorway as she approaches a spicemonger's cart a half-block distant. She's wearing a different dress, a blue and white jalabiya. It's as threadbare as the last but well made, with fine stitching, the sort a woman of means might once have worn. Her black keffiyeh lies loosely around her head, but oddly, as if she wasn't born to it and had only recently started wearing one. She glances warily along the street as the plump fruit seller uses her pewter scoop to fill a burlap sack with dried wolfberry.

Brama's curiosity rises. And for good reason. Wolfberry has a pleasant enough flavor, but the aftertaste is bitter as oversteeped tea. For this reason the fruit is not favored by most market-goers in Sharakhai, but it sells well enough in the Shallows, mainly for its ability to help ease the lows that go hand in hand with an addiction to black lotus. The girl shows none of the effects of addiction herself. Her hands don't shake as she passes over a small handful of copper, nor are her lips bloodless, and her eyes are anything but sallow. There is, however, an undeniable weight on her shoulders. A sense of worry. A natural reaction, I suppose, if someone she loves is deep in the throes of withdrawal, but that wouldn't explain why she's constantly looking up and down the street as though she's worried about being discovered.

As it did the other day when Brama first spotted her, a play of lights flit about her, tumbling through the air. They look like a chromatic flock of cressetwing moths, mesmerizing as they brighten in the shadows and fade in the shafts of morning sunlight.

They have never failed to amaze me. And it's no different for Brama. He stares, rapt. But as the wind-tossed flecks of light slowly disappear, it bothers him greatly. He's suddenly convinced she will die. Brama has no way of knowing, but the lights never remain with a single soul for long, and I have no way of sharing this with him, not until he summons me again. Truth be told, though, I don't know that I would even if he did. His indecision glows like a beacon fire, a thing somehow pleasing to my muted senses. It's clear he wants to go to her, but what would he say? He knows by now, or at least suspects, that her fate is entwined with his, but the likelihood of scaring her with but a word is a near certainty.

No sooner does the thought cross his mind than the girl spies him in the doorway of the shisha den. The sheer depth of terror seen in her eyes convinces me of two things: first, she's afraid of being found, and second, she isn't sure *who* might be hunting her, else why be so frightened of a man she's never met?

Wrapping her keffiyeh tighter around her face, she snatches the bag of wolfberries from the spicemonger and sets off briskly down a different street than she'd taken here.

Brama, feeling more than foolish, debates whether

to follow. *What would I tell her?* he muses. *Hello. I'm Brama. I've seen lights around you. We're fated to meet.* He laughs at the very thought, but then notices a man exiting the street the girl had taken here. He wears beaten trousers and a dirty, sweat-stained shirt. He's short and lithe as a willow, and moves with the gait of a man used to masking the sound of his footfalls. He weaves past two men carrying a dusty, rolled-up carpet, then follows the girl.

He is the one she fears. Brama and I both know it.

Another block up, where the traffic grows thicker, the girl glances back. She looks straight past the man following her to Brama, and then ducks into a winding street that will take her toward the heart of the Knot, a maze of narrow alleys where one might easily lose pursuers if one knows the paths to take. No doubt she does, but she doesn't see the man turn and sprint along the street closest to Brama, an avenue that could easily be used, assuming one moves fast enough, to cut her off.

After a moment's indecision, Brama draws his knife from its sheath along his forearm and sprints after him. Brama takes more care than I've given him credit for. I forget that he grew up on these streets, that he once prowled the city's rooftops. He moves deceptively fast, and uses the crowd to his advantage, hugging the edge of the street, so that when the man glances back, Brama slows to a walking pace and angles toward a ramshackle chandler's shop. He reaches for the candles hanging like sausages from a length of twine as if they were exactly what he'd been after.

The man moves on, and Brama resumes the chase, moving faster now, nearing the place where the angled avenue the girl took rejoins the street they both now race along. Ahead lies a square where the buildings lean precariously, a tangled courtyard of sorts, formed and held in place by a crisscross of rooms and roofs and makeshift bridges built on the shoulders of the original structures. The man steps into the shadow of a bath house awning as the girl appears ahead, moving briskly but warily.

Brama creeps along the rough stone of the bathhouse behind the waiting man, his confidence and nervousness mixing to create an intoxicating brew. I, on the other hand, sense something amiss, the sort of worry that buzzes at the base of the skull like a trapped hornet. Had I my proper form I could discern what it was with a moment of concentration, but trapped as I am all I can do is to try to warn Brama.

One moment I'm pushing Brama to be wary, and

the next, Brama's senses flare as the sound of pounding footfalls nears. Brama dodges to one side as someone barrels into him from behind. Pain bright burns along his side and the back of his ribs.

Brama loses his knife as he tries to break his fall against the dusty street. He scrabbles away from his attacker, a man with a wild beard, wilder hair, and a ratty thawb—a beggar from the looks of him, but I can already see he's no beggar. His teeth are clean. His hair and beard, though messy, are anything but grimy. He'd pass for a beggar at ten paces, but to my eye the disguise is plain as a mummer's mask. Whether Brama senses the same, I do not know, but given the man's aquiline nose and high brow, I have few doubts he's the ally of the Malasani who waits in the shadows.

As Brama and his attacker wrestle across the dusty courtyard, those who'd been loitering or walking along the street back away. Brama takes another cut along his forearm from the slim, straight knife. They roll into a trash heap and his assailant pounces on top of Brama. The man stabs the knife at Brama's neck. Brama snatches the man's wrist, holding the knife at bay. Then he rams a knee into the attacker's ribs, and rolls out from under him, twisting the man's wrist until he drops the blade on the dirt.

As the man Brama was following rushes to help his comrade, Brama rises and backs away, spreading his attention between the two men. Wisely, his opponents fan out, and soon it's plain to see they're used to fighting with one another. The smaller man darts in. The moment Brama turns to face him, the wild-haired one rushes forward. In one sinuous move, he throws Brama over his hip and slams him to the ground.

Blood pours from the knife wound along Brama's back. It flows along his forearm as well. For me it is like a fount from the gods, the very source of the essence of life. I would drink of it if I could, so heady is its scent, but a wall stands between us. Yet it doesn't have to be so. If Brama would simply accept the power I've offered him… I offer it again as the beggar straddles him, as he holds the tip of his slim knife against Brama's neck. For the first time since being trapped within this gem, I worry. There's no telling what these men might do when they find the sapphire hidden beneath Brama's shirt. *Please*, I beg Brama, *take but a sip of my power. Take it, and save yourself.*

Brama, however, remains resolute. I feel the revulsion and hatred he holds for me. For the first time, however, I feel temptation as well.

The man kneels on Brama's chest. "Who are you?"

he asked, his Malasani accent thick.

"I am but a relic of a man," Brama replies. "A ruin."

The Malasani grins. "Even ruins can be buried, so I ask you once again—"

He never finishes those words, for just then a length of wood appears, piercing the man's neck with a sound like a hook piercing a pig's neck before it's hung for slaughter. Yellow fletching graces one end of the shaft of wood, a bloody broadhead the other.

The man's eyes go wide. He coughs wetly, spitting warm blood across Brama's face. He tries to pull the bolt free, but stops when his own blood spurts in a torrent across Brama's shoulder. His jaw works, as if he's still trying to ask his question of Brama—who are you?—but then Brama rolls him aside and scrambles to a stand.

Ten paces away stands a man in a stained nightdress, one foot in the stirrup of a crossbow as he strains to lever the string back. He hardly looks as though he can keep his feet, but he manages to lock the string in place. With shaking arms, he lifts the crossbow and sets a fresh bolt into the channel, but before he can lift it and aim, Brama's second attacker sprints away, darting and into a tea house that had just opened its doors. As the tea house's proprietor shouts in surprise after him, the lanky man in his night clothes lifts the tip of the crossbow until it's aimed at Brama's chest. The girl stands behind him, a slim knife to hand, looking like she knows how to use it.

"A question was posed to you," the man says, crossbow poised and ready. He speaks Sharakhani well, but with noticeable notes of a Malasani nobleman's upbringing. He glances at Brama's attacker, who's fallen still, staring at the sky as blood drains weakly around the shaft of the crossbow bolt sticking out of his neck. "As he seems indisposed, perhaps you would be so kind as to give me the answer in his stead."

"I am no one," Brama replies.

"You're a liar," he spits back, and raises the butt of the crossbow to his shoulder.

The lights have begun to swirl around the girl once more. Her eyes are round with worry. She keeps looking back over her shoulder, toward the cluttered alley that led to another part of the Shallows. She's deferring to the crossbowman, a malnourished man with sunken, jaundiced eyes and hollowed cheeks, but she clearly wishes to leave, to run, to hide themselves in the city. As she swallows, perhaps stifling something she was about to say, the lights around her move to encapsulate the man as well, though the effects aren't nearly as bright as they are around her.

I can feel Brama's desire to leave, though he isn't so desperate as this girl. He wants to return to his room and hide from the outside world, but his curiosity over the lights, the girl, is too strong. "I am a man born and raised in these very streets," Brama finally says. "I see who comes and who goes. I've seen her"—he points to the girl—"come here, bright-eyed, worried. And today I saw that man, the one you just let get away, follow her. I know when there's trouble about, and I didn't want it to befall her."

After a moment's pause, the man lowers the crossbow a fraction. "These are your streets then? You're like to the Silver Spears, beholden to the Kings of Sharakhai?"

Brama spits onto the dirt. "No. But this is my home, and I would protect it."

He looks Brama up and down, his eyes lingering on Brama's scars. "A tattered prince."

Brama nods. "A tattered prince."

"In the future"—he begins backing away, grabbing the girl's arm as he goes—"if you happen upon me or my sister, you'll be sure to walk the other way."

"Wait." Brama takes a step forward, but stops when the man brings the crossbow up. "Who are you?"

The man merely backs away, crossbow in one hand, the girl's wrist in the other, then he and the girl turn and jog down the street. Soon they're lost from sight, and the bystanders, who'd been watching warily, one by one lose interest and return to their day.

The following morning, an insistent pounding shakes the door of Brama's room above the tannery. The smells in the air are horrible, acrid, like horse piss, but it keeps people away, and that's all he really cares about. As he rolls out of bed and stares at the door, the memories of the fight in the streets play across his mind. He wears only his trousers and bandages around his wounds. He probes them gently, finds them to be healing faster than he's expected. A gift from me, though I don't tell him so.

When the pounding comes again, it's more insistent. "Open this sodding door, Brama!" a deep voice shouts.

Brama pulls on a shirt, takes up his curved kenshar from the bedside table, and unsheathes it. He stares at the sapphire, my sapphire, and a vision of the man he'd fought in the streets flashes through his mind. As he slips the necklace over his head and stuffs it into his shirt, I feel something I've been working toward since becoming trapped in this gem. I was beginning to think it would never happen, but the relief in Brama, even if slight, is clear.

Relief…toward me, the one who'd tortured him mercilessly for months on end. He doesn't trust me—I doubt he'll ever truly trust me—but he's beginning to rely on me, which is just as good. He knows well the power embodied in me. He knows he can use it. Have I not offered it a thousand times and a thousand times more? He has but to say the word. It's clear he hasn't yet made up his mind about accepting my offer, but this is a delicious first step. Like a wedge being hammered into wood, I'm certain it won't be long before his resolve cracks.

Brama steps lightly toward the door. For all my smug pleasure, I grow worried as he reaches for the latch. I'm vulnerable, beholden to a mortal, a thing that infuriates me when I dwell on it overlong. It makes me wonder what I've done to displease my lord Goezhen, but I also know it could grow worse. Well worse. There's no telling whose hands I might fall into were Brama to lose me or fall to an enemy's blade. No telling what they might do if my presence within the gem is detected. In Brama, at least, I know the sort of man he is. Thus far, he's taken the utmost care not to reveal my nature.

When Brama opens the door, he finds not the assassin, but a towering man with one hunched shoulder and a deep, ragged scar running over his left eye.

Brama's voice is gravel and stones as he speaks the man's name. "Kymbril."

One side of the scarred giant's mouth crooks upward. "Didn't know if you'd remember me, boy."

"I'm not a boy." Brama looks him up and down. "And you're a bit hard to forget."

Kymbril stares over Brama's shoulder into the room. One of his eyes is colored shit brown, and the other, the one with the scar, is a grey-blue, like the overcast skies of desert winter. It's what earned Kymbril his nickname, the Mismatched Man. "You going to invite me in?"

"I'm busy."

"Doing what?"

"Sleeping."

Kymbril grins his toothy grin; his mismatched eyes shine like the edge of a knife. "You're a joker, you are. Be careful it doesn't earn you a missing tooth or two. Wouldn't want that pretty smile of yours ruined."

He bulls forward, daring Brama to stop him. Brama lets him pass, then closes the door behind him. Like a forge's flame fanned by the bellows, I feel Brama's worry being stoked by Kymbril's presence. Surprisingly, though, it's more about the girl than it is about himself. He knows as well as I do this visit has something to do with her. Sliding the sheath back over the kenshar's blade, he lofts it toward the tabletop. It clatters across the wood and falls to the floor with a thud.

Brama sits on the room's lone chair, leaning into it as if he were some duty-ridden king preparing to suffer through the day's final petition. Kymbril, meanwhile, takes in the room, examining the table, the pile of clothes in the corner, the space between the bed and the wall.

"Get on with it," Brama says.

Kymbril continues his inspection as if Brama hadn't spoken. When he seems satisfied, he sits on Brama's bed as if the room were his, and rests elbows on knees, the way a dear friend might before imparting unfortunate news. "Already warned you once, boy. There'll be no warning the third time."

Brama says nothing, but I can feel the desire in him for Kymbril to do something. Anything. The rage he has for me and the pain he'd endured when he'd been mine is now a deep well Brama draws on when it suits him. Such things would crush most men, but in Brama it has become the fuel he uses to make his own fire burn brighter. It's saved him more than once, but it's also landed him into trouble.

"Yesterday," Kymbril begins, "you were seen speaking with a man named Nehir."

"I don't know anyone named Nehir."

"Thin. Handsome bloke, but has the look of the reek about him. I believe he was holding a crossbow on you?"

"I don't know anything about him."

Kymbril nods as if Brama is being perfectly reasonable. "Then why were you talking with him?"

"A few men were following him. Didn't like the look of them, so…we had words."

Kymbril smiles genuinely. "Had words… I like that." The big man frowns, lost in thought. "You seen them around before? Nehir and his little sister, Jax?"

Brama brightens upon learning her name. He savors it a moment. Jax. "Never saw Nehir before that day. Didn't even know his name until you said it just now. But I've seen the girl here and there."

Kymbril waits for more, then frowns when Brama doesn't continue. "That's your story?"

"That's my story."

Kymbril nods. "Very well. Now I'm going to tell you a story, Brama. And when I'm done I'm going to ask you a question, and you're going to answer it for me." He pauses, licks his lips while staring at the ceiling, as if ordering the events in his mind. "A few months back our young man, Nehir, shows up in one of my parlors. Smokes a while. Some expensive tabbaq, I'm told. Then he gets raging drunk on our finest wine, which, I readily admit, is not all that fine to begin with. He starts telling everyone who'll listen how he's a lord of Malasan, how his holding had been stolen from him by a neighboring duke, how he'd been chased from his homeland here to Sharakhai. Vowed revenge, he did. On the lord who killed his family. On those who stood by and let it happen. Even swore he'd kill the king of Malasan himself if he wasn't restored to his family seat. Everyone humors him because he's buying araq, wine, whatever they want, but they're all grinning behind their cups, and when he leaves, they're laughing before the door even slams home.

"A few days pass, and Nehir stumbles in through that same door, already two sheets gone, saying much the same thing. He buys more for the house, starts waxing on about knives in the night and revenge against the mountain lords of Malasan, but this time, a little girl shows up and leads him stumbling back into the streets. And here we come to the interesting part, Brama, so pay attention. Not a week passes before a man from Malasan darkens the doorway of that very same parlor. Thin man. Calm. As likely to knife you as smile. You know the type. He asks a few questions. Drops a coin or two in the process. He wants to know about Nehir—what he looks like, whether the parlor maid had seen him since, where he might be found now. This news drifts to me, as you might imagine. Didn't think much of it at the time, but I had my best man, Maru, check into it."

Brama knew Maru. Everyone in the Shallows did. He was a pit fighter once, but he'd found the competition too equitable, so he left and joined Kymbril's gang in search of friendlier sands over which to sail. He'd since built a reputation for being as vicious as he was skilled with a blade.

"Maru found neither Nehir nor the girl, so I put it from my mind. Figured they'd moved on. But then, lo and behold, not two weeks later word comes that a few of my regular patrons aren't looking for reek with the same sort of fervor they once had. Some stop buying altogether. Makes a man wonder, that does. Makes him worry. So I send Maru out sniffing, and what does he find? That someone's been funneling Malasani black into the Shallows without my leave."

Brama's curiosity is piqued, as is mine. Until this point he thought Kymbril had sent those men after Nehir. He thought he'd be dealing with a loss of one of Kymbril's own men at Brama's hands. But now it's clear there's a third player. He might just come out and ask it—Who was the man? You must know something!—but mortals have a curious way of filling silences and revealing more than they mean to, so Brama silently waits.

"You can imagine"—Kymbril reaches down and scuffs bits of dirt off the tops of his worn leather boots—"the sort of black cloud hanging over me when I found out. You can imagine the sort of imaginative phrases that came out of my demure fucking mouth. I've been looking for Nehir ever since. I'm not too much of a man that I can't admit I've been thwarted thus far. Maru's normally quite good at rooting such men out, but Nehir's a tricky one. Then I hear something strange. Do you know what it was, Brama?"

Brama shakes his head.

"I hear that some man riddled with enough scars to make a soldier blush gets into it with two men chasing

Nehir and Jax like hounds on a brace of wounded hares. That true, Brama? You following those men?"

"I was."

Kymbril nods, neither pleased nor displeased. "Thought so." His brow creases as if he's working out the final pieces of a puzzle but can't quite get to them to fit. "You can imagine how a man in my position might wonder why you'd do such a thing. Why you'd protect them. Doesn't seem to be a reason. Unless…" He purses his lips, the picture of a man lost in thought, then nods as if the last of the pieces had fallen into place and the painting was now clear. "Unless you have a vested interest. You know that term, Brama? A vested interest?"

A manic gaze had replaced the look of sufferance in Kymbril's ill-matched eyes, and the tightness in Brama is building. He's ready for anything from Kymbril. As am I.

"A vested interest means you protected him because he means something to you. Let's say Nehir was your brother. You'd protect him then, wouldn't you? Or if he was paying you. Then you'd certainly protect him. Tell me it isn't so."

"I never met him before that day, Kymbril. I swear it."

The muscles along Kymbril's shoulders bunch. "He swears it." He stands and stabs a knotted branch of a finger at Brama's chest. "When I was your age, I was already carving out my territory, right here in the Knot. I took it from a man who was as cruel a bastard as I've ever come across. But while I was coming into my prime, he was going rheumy with age. He was worried more about the tea that helped his gout than the men who ran his reek for him. Do my eyes look rheumy to you, Brama?" He cracks the knuckles on one hand loudly, then does the same to the other. "Do I look like I couldn't take down a bone crusher with one fist?"

"You are the envy of all who survey you. As fit a man as I've ever seen."

With blinding speed, Kymbril grabs Brama by the throat and drives him backward. The chair tips over and Brama falls to the floor. He doesn't move a muscle to stop Kymbril, even though I offer him all the power he needs. I am more incensed at Kymbril's actions than I ever thought I'd be. Coming here to Brama's home and pretending he owns all he lays his eyes on…

"Are you working for Nehir?" Kymbril asks, his breath heavy with lemon and garlic. "Be careful how you answer, now. Take your time. It could mean your life."

His hand is around Brama's neck, squeezing hard enough to bruise, pinching Brama's windpipe so tightly his breath comes in choking gasps. Brama shows no pain, though, nor does he flinch, not even when Kymbril lifts him by the neck and slams him down onto the warped floorboards.

"I work for no one," Brama replies.

"Not even me?" A threat. An offer.

"Especially not for you."

Kymbril's laughs a deep rumble of a laugh. His eyes drift down to Brama's neck, where the sapphire in its dirty leather wrapping has spilled from his shirt. "Man could stand to make a pretty pile of coin, he sold a thing like that."

"I could never sell this, Kymbril."

"Oh? Why's that?"

"After I fucked your mum every which way but sideways, she handed it to me with a smile so bright that tears came to my eyes. Told me never to part with it as she placed it in my hands."

Kymbril stares, eyes crazed, even a bit fearful, as if he can't figure out why Brama isn't more scared of him. But then his face softens and he laughs, a loud affair, the sort the drug lord is known for. "You're a twisted little fuck, you are." Then he shoves Brama away, stands, and walks out, chuckling, as if Brama hadn't just denied him something he very much wanted.

A short while later, Brama stares into a brass mirror hung above the wash basin. His room is dark, but there's a candle on the table below the mirror, lighting the carpet-weave pattern of his scars in a ghastly pallor. "Did you know he would come?"

"I'm no god, Brama. I cannot see the future."

He chooses his next words with care. "I need to find the girl."

I stare back at him, calm for all the anticipation that's boiling up inside me. Even though I'm bound, even though I'm imprisoned and beholden to Brama, the things Kymbril revealed have lit a fire in me. Kymbril is now a part of the light that surrounds the girl, Jax, as is her brother, Nehir, as is the assassin chasing them. I know it is so. I just don't know how as yet, or why. But that is all part of the wonder of this gift given me by Goezhen. Like a flower unfolding, it changes every time but is no less beautiful for it.

"Why would you care if she lives or dies?" I ask.

"You've never even spoken to her."

He knows I can sense his thoughts and still he lies. "I don't care for her."

"Do you not?"

His face has begun to flush. "She's being preyed upon by her brother and by the people of her homeland. Soon Kymbril will have her, and when he does, he won't let her go until he's wrung every last copper from her. And then he'll give her back to the desert with a knife across the throat."

"And you won't allow it?"

"You know I won't." His words are a nod to how he was preyed upon by me. A bit of that dark time flits through our minds, and I feel his resolve harden, his anger toward me growing in the bargain. "Tell me how I can find her."

I reach out to him. "You know you have but to take my hand."

"No." He recoils. "Lead me to her."

In the mirror, my expression saddens. "Alas, in my current state that is well beyond me. Had I true form, however..."

Brama's face pinches in anger. From a shelf beneath the basin he takes out a small lead box. "Wait," I say, but Brama ignores me, placing the necklace inside it.

"Wait! You may torture me if you wish, but it changes nothing!"

The lid closes, and all goes black.

I feel nothing. Not Brama. Not the tiny room he's chosen to live in. Not the tannery nor the Shallows beyond. None of Sharakhai. None of the desert. Not even the heat, nor the sky, nor the endless sands. I know not how Brama found this secret, but it is my one true fear, my one true weakness, to be utterly parted from all I've come to love.

I feel myself falling. Down a deep hole I drift, and the farther I plummet, the more I worry that I'll never be able to return even if Brama were to open the box. It is one of the few ways we, the ehrekh, can die. Does Brama know this? I hope not. By the gods who walk the earth, I hope not. Far worse than the isolation is the sense of being undone, of leaving this place, never to return. I will never go to the farther fields as Brama will when he dies. Lacking the blood of the elder gods, I will live in this realm until my final hour, and then I will simply be gone, like smoke from a candle snuffed. It is a fear I have always harbored, but now it consumes me.

Time passes—how much I cannot tell—but finally, blessedly, the lid of the box opens, and Brama takes me up once more.

I stare at him in the mirror, my dark skin cast golden in the wavering brass. "I cannot find her! Not unless you will it!"

"I do will it," he says.

"But you must accept what I give!"

He lowers the sapphire. "Never."

"Then you will not find her and all that you've predicted will come to pass! Save her if you would, Brama Junayd'ava. You have but to take my hand."

For a moment, the gem remains, hovering above the leaden box. He is lost in the memories of our time together. Part of him wants to be done with me once and for all, but there is another part that wonders at the things he might do were he to accept the power I could give him.

I whisper to him, "You could rule this city if you so wished."

A heartbeat passes. Then another. Slowly, Brama lifts the gem from the box and stares at my beaten reflection once more. "How?"

"Welcome me," I say to him. "Welcome me, and use the gifts I lay at your very doorstep. You have but to say the word, and I will be returned to my prison. All is at your will. But make no mistake. Your very form and frame is necessary. You must open yourself to me."

He stares into my eyes, and I know he's already decided. The dread from moments ago lingers, but for the first time since being trapped between the facets of this sapphire, I feel like I've taken a step closer to setting myself free—not because of Brama, but because of the girl. She is the key, though I cannot yet say how. The path the fates have laid for me is often clear only well after the lights have first been shown.

"Very well," Brama says, and indeed he welcomes me.

I approach, and he blinks, once, twice. When he opens his eyes the third time, his view of the world has changed. He sees more. Motes of magic drifting on the subtle breezes within this dingy room in the slums of Sharakhai. He hears more. Echoes of life and death and anger and lust. The very breath of the first gods falls upon his skin, making it tingle here, then there, then deep inside him.

He walks to the door. Opens it. Takes the stairs down and enters the street. So many scents are on the wind. The young. The old. Lovers. Sworn enemies.

"What now?" Brama says to the first star in the sky.

"You walk the city."

And so he does, the twinkling lights of fate brightening as he goes.

Near the edge of the Shallows sprawl five mountainous buildings, the constituent parts of an ancient tenement built hundreds of years ago as a barracks for a looming war with Qaimir. The buildings show their age: their amber stone crumbling, arched windows chipped away by more recent inhabitants, graffiti along the ground floor written in paint or blood or shit. The slumlord who owns them cares little about its outward appearance, nor does he care how poorly the interiors are treated; one need only enter any of the edifices to see the truth of that: refuse in the halls, holes in the walls between rooms, the unyielding smell of piss and unventilated cooking—humanity squeezed to the breaking point. No, the lord of this manor cares only that his rent collectors are able to sweep through with their enforcers and gather the handful of copper khet owed from each and every room at the beginning of each and every week.

More interesting to Brama is the sheer number of entrances and exits to this gargantuan complex. Like a tribe of desert titans, each building has eight scalloped archways that disgorge or ingest its inhabitants. Each has four courtyards as well, with exits to the north and south. Above, makeshift walkways string between these and the neighboring buildings, making up one small part of the sprawling rooftop neighborhood the Shallows is famed for. No doubt there are even a few underground tunnels leading to and from this place.

It all makes for the perfect place for Nehir and Jax to hide. And so it was with little surprise that the lights led Brama here. They dissipate, however, when he nears the buildings, and though he's walked their circumference several times over the past few days, he still hasn't found her.

"Why?" he asked me that first night in his beaten brass mirror.

"The fates are fickle friends," I told him. "The path is not always clear. It can become clouded by others who hold power or control the fate of those involved. It can become dulled by the sheer press of humanity in Sharakhai. My guess, however, is that for the time being, the fates have found other, more interesting baubles to play with. That or they've simply not decided what to do with you."

Or, more accurately, me.

Brama seemed unsatisfied, but it is the plain truth,

and the only answer I could give. I worry over it as much as he does, perhaps more. I feel as though this story, however it unfolds, is a test on the part of the fates, a way to offer me a path back into their good graces. For all my power, for all the centuries I've spent living in every corner of the Great Shangazi, I am as much in control of my own destiny as Brama is of his.

Sundown nears as Brama waits. The light splashing against the buildings fades, burns red. And then Jax comes rushing from an alley into the nearest of the tenements' tall buildings. She slips through a darkened archway and is gone, but Brama is already on her trail. He heads inside but promptly loses her to a stairwell twenty paces along the narrow hallway. Tenement dwellers watch Brama pass by their doorless entries. Some peek out from behind blankets hung across their cramped rooms, or lift their heads from their meals to stare through strings of beads. Some even make love, but it doesn't do to lower one's guard in the Shallows, so they watch him pass, then return to their rutting.

Brama hurries up the stairwell, glancing along the hallway of the second story, then the third. Finding both empty—of sparkling girls, at least—he continues to the fourth floor. At the end of the dirty corridor, a gutted window shows a sky of brilliant mauve gilded in the orange light of the setting sun. Just short of the window, he sees the silhouette of a girl slipping inside a room. Brama approaches carefully, pausing near the doorway, which has a beaten old carpet hung across it. The sound of shuffling comes from within, then the rhythmic thump of a mortar and pestle, accompanied by sniffing sounds. Other sounds rise up all around in this cramped hive of humanity, but lying in the interstitial spaces between them is a sibilant hiss, the rasp of wet breath. The scent of black lotus laces the air, an earthy, floral smell that lingers, especially when one has been smoking it for as long as Nehir apparently has.

As Brama reaches to move the carpet aside, the mortar goes silent; the carpet is flung wide and the girl rushes out, knife to hand. She presses the knife to Brama's throat until he's against the wall behind him. She stares at him, her brows pinched in confusion. She expected someone else—the assassin, most likely, assuming Kymbril's story is true.

She starts to speak, then glances back, pulls the carpet back into place to hide the sight of Nehir lying in a hammock slung between the mudbrick walls. "What do you want with us?" she asks in a thick Malasani accent.

Brama pauses to think. "I don't know. I only wish

to help."

She stares at Brama's scars, clearly revolted, clearly scared. "We need no help from you."

"Yes you do. The world is closing in around you. It won't be long now before Kymbril has you."

She frowns, her brow furrowing. "Who's Kymbril?"

It's clear then how woefully incomplete her understanding of the situation is. She knows some—else why hide in this place and cover her tracks so carefully?—but she understands neither the nature of the danger nor its immediacy.

Before Brama can reply, a filthy man wearing only his small clothes approaches along the hallway. His eyes are dark and haunted, his malnourished ribs like ripples on a windswept pond. He carries something, a single silver six-piece that he holds with both hands toward Jax as if it's meant to save his own mother.

"Go on!" Jax shouts. And when he doesn't, she screams at him, "There's nothing for you here!"

He remains, mouth opening and closing uselessly. He shuffles one step forward, holding the sliver of a silver coin out further.

"Go!"

Finally the man leaves, the sound of his footsteps replaced by a choking sound from inside the room. Jax's eyes go wide. She bats the carpet aside and bursts into the room. Brama holds the carpet wide as she sinks to the floor by her brother's side. His eyelids flutter. His body convulses, rocking the hammock slung between the walls of the narrow room.

Beneath the hammock sits a grimy shisha, its frayed black tube snaking across the floor. Next to the shisha is the mortar and pestle. She tosses the pestle aside, spraying some of the red paste onto the floor, then uses her fingers to scoop up some of the crushed wolfberry. "Nehir," she whispers. "Nehir, take this." She smears as much of the red paste into his mouth as she can, making him look as though his gums were bleeding. "Swallow it!"

He doesn't respond. The embrace of the black lotus is already on him, and it's drawing him deeper and deeper. It will never let him go. As we watch with all the impotence of babes, his spasms begin to slow. His eyes roll up in his head. His breath comes slower, more shallowly.

Jax turns to Brama, her eyes brimming with tears. "Do something!"

Brama stands silent, peering around the room. In a corner lies a bowl of water with a rag folded carefully along one edge. He steps across the room, drops down in front of the bowl, and stares into the reflection. "What can I do?"

Slowly, the smooth black skin of my face forms in the white bowl of water. Twin horns furl backward. Black spines replace Brama's curly hair. "Little enough," I say. "Give him comfort. Give him more of the reek to ease his flight."

"You know that isn't what I mean."

"My dear Brama," I say, reaching out to his mind, "if you wish for my help, you know what you must do."

Brama stares into the water, his worries roiling inside him.

Jax, hands clutched to her throat, steps closer and stares at the bowl. "Who are you talking to?"

Brama ignores her. "Do it," he says to me.

Do it. Allow me to take his form, at least for a time, and to some small degree. It's doubtful I can do anything more than help with Nehir—the narrow tie between us will not allow me to do all that I might wish—but we both know that the more I'm allowed to do this, the more dangerous it becomes for Brama.

When Brama first accepted the gem that contains me, I thought surely he would use it to bring himself fortune or to grant himself long life. It would take time, surely, for our dealings before that point were anything but kind to Brama, but so often when mortals gain power, their only wish is to gain more. Brama hadn't wished for that, though. He'd squirreled me away, sometimes in the lead box, other times beneath his mattress, other times within his shirt. He'd never sought power.

Until now.

"There is a cost," I tell Brama. "You will be required to act in this as well. Your body must suffer in his place."

"I don't care if I suffer." And he means it. I've felt the disregard he has for his own life, the pain that befalls him. I feel it even now.

"Very well."

"Please," Jax says, and then goes silent as Brama stands. She watches as he steps to her brother's side. Watches as Brama takes his hand. In this moment, Brama lowers his guard. It feels not like the opening of a door, but more of a nod, a bow to me. It is all I need.

I forge a connection between Brama and Nehir, a bond that begins as a thread but strengthens, braiding and multiplying until the two men are intertwined. Their minds are still unique, but their forms intermingle. Their hearts. Their bodies. These are what I care about now. Slowly, the effects of the reek are drawn from Nehir and into Brama. His body carries that terrible burden, leaving Nehir breathing easier, his eyes less restless. Nehir's shaking quells and he slips into a deeper sleep, and the touch of the black lotus takes Brama. He stumbles backward, falls against the nearby wall. He slips down until his head is resting against the corner of the room.

He hears the sounds of the tenement, which are wondrous and terrifying in equal amounts. The cry of a babe brightens until it becomes the touch of Tulathan herself. The sound of a man's feet treading barefoot is the tread of an assassin. Jax squats before him. She speaks, but Brama cannot hear her words. She shakes him, gently at first, then violently. But Brama doesn't care. Jax is nothing to him, merely one small part in the grand canvas of sounds and scents that grow and shrink like the aeons of life and death in a forest, all experienced in the blink of an eye.

Down, down Brama drifts, into the forest, the landscape ever changing. Brama wanders through the trees, through the hills, wondering where his place in this new world might be.

When Brama wakes, his head feels as though it's being pounded like a cubit stone in the quarry. He lies on the floor of the same small tenement room, drool slipping from his mouth, pooling against the red-tiled floor beneath him. As he lifts himself up and props himself against the wall, the pounding becomes so terrible, stars form in his eyes. Only after long minutes of breathing and allowing the storm to pass does Brama realize he is alone. He stares at the empty hammock, takes in the rest of the room, which holds considerably less clutter than it had before he'd freed Nehir.

Hardly surprising, Brama thinks.

Still, the betrayal stings, and for a time all he can manage to do is hold his head in his hands and try to press away the pain.

I'm distanced from his bodily feelings, but not completely so—I helped him to lift the effects of the black lotus, after all. The way his body grieves reminds me of the mortals with whom I've bonded in the past. This is vastly different, though. Every time before now, I'd been the one in control. I felt what I wanted to feel, did what I wanted to do with the form I'd taken, and it was often wondrous. Now, the crystal makes me beholden to the one who holds it, and I feel so much less. Brama is duller than he might have been. Less interesting to me. If only I might find a way to free myself from this prison once and for all.

Brama stares at the shisha. The rank smell disgusts him, but there is a part of him that wants to walk among the trees of the forest once more. It's a small part, to be sure, but distinct. It was surely due to how addicted to the reek Nehir had been. Brama is strong enough in body and spirit to withstand it and not become shackled to the drug, but were he to continue to do this, he could easily succumb to the desire.

Brama's gaze drifts to the empty hammock. "I should have let him die."

"Perhaps you should have," comes a heavy voice.

Brama turns his head, wincing from the pain it brings, to find a bald man standing in the doorway, pushing the carpet aside. It was Maru, Kymbril's man. He steps inside the room, and the carpet flaps closed behind him. Brama reaches for his knife, but finds it gone. Maru gives the room a cursory inspection, then kneels before Brama, a curved and nicked kenshar held easily in one hand.

He cranes his neck and runs the knife blade over his stubbly neck, scratching an itch. "Kymbril's going to be awfully disappointed in you."

"Why's that?" Brama asks.

Maru points the tip of the knife at Brama's chest. "Told him you didn't know Nehir. Said you worked for no one."

Brama thinks back, frowns. "You were there, weren't you, outside the door?"

Maru shrugs his broad shoulders. "He may not act like it, but Kymbril's a careful man." Brama opens his mouth to speak, but Maru talks over him. "Now let's get a few things straight, you and me. First, before I leave this room, you're going to tell me where I can find Nehir and that little bitch sister of his. Second, at no point in this conversation will you tell me that you don't know. Third, and this is the most important point, Brama, so bend your ear. Third, Kymbril may be a careful man, but I'm not." He holds the kenshar up for Brama to see. He stares over it, just above its well-honed edge, into Brama's eyes. "I'm a messy man. A persistent man. I'm a jackal who's gone too hungry to care about leopards or lions or whatever the fuck else might be standing in front of me."

Since Brama escaped my attentions, he's had a streak in him that seeks out conflict, that desires pain. Something broke in him while he was in my care, and I can feel it inside him now, rising to stand before Maru like a defiant child before a charging destrier. Worse is the fact that I see a darkness forming around Maru, the sort that comes when something threatens me.

Beware, Brama! Take my hand!

To my amazement, Brama does reach for me, but in that moment his hand also grasps absently for the sapphire beneath his shirt. Maru's hand darts forward and snatches the leather cord around Brama's neck. He yanks it, snapping the cord, taking the sapphire that holds me with it. My sight, my hearing, so dependent on Brama, both dim, but I can still hear Maru as he says, "None of that," holding the gemstone up.

He slips it into his pocket, his eyes still on Brama. Brama chooses that moment to kick Maru in the knee. Maru, however, for all his bulk, is a sinuous man. His leg snaps back, dulling the blow. Then, quick as a cobra, he grabs Brama by the neck, slams him against the rough stone wall, and drops him to the floor.

"Now." Maru is close, his dark eyes intense, his kahve-laden breath strong and rank. He holds the knife between Brama's legs, pressing the blade up against his crotch. Brama grips Maru's wrist, keeping the knife at bay, but only just. "Choose carefully, Brama. I'm only going to ask you one more time. Where's that Malasani cunt?"

"Crawled up one of the Kings' arses," Brama shoots back. "Which is good news for you, Maru. You only have to shove your head up a dozen of them to find her."

"Bad choice, boy."

Maru draws the knife upward. Brama, jaw clenched tight, teeth bared, tries to stop him, but as weak as he is from the effects of the lotus, it's a losing battle from the start.

The scene slowly fades—the sights, the sounds, the smells. It represents, perhaps, an uncorrectable shift in my fate, a poorly chosen path. Suddenly the scene brightens. Maru's breathing is a wet rasp in Brama's ears. The knife's edge burns bright between Brama's legs, searing his skin.

There's a hollow thump, and Maru goes slack. His weight falls across Brama, and Brama shoves him away. Jax is there, standing over the two of them holding a heavy, blood-stained ewer above her head, ready to strike again. She's shivering, panting, staring at the bloody gouge on the back of Maru's head.

Brama levers himself out from under Maru and comes to a stand. Jax drops the ewer, which thuds against the floor. After taking takes Maru's knife and slipping it under his belt, Brama reaches into Maru's shirt pocket, takes back the necklace, and ties it around his neck.

"Nehir wouldn't let me stay," Jax says, an apology of sorts.

Brama only shrugs. "I mightn't have, either, were I him."

"I'm sorry. I know you saved us, but he's scared. He has his wits about him now, though. He has you to thank, does he not?"

Brama nods.

"It was the gem?"

"In a manner of speaking."

The girl takes a deep breath. Someone further down the hall begins shouting at their child. Jax turns and stares wide-eyed at the carpet over her doorway, but as their argument quells, she turns back to Brama. "I haven't a right to ask, but I need help. We need help, even if Nehir won't admit it."

Brama looks down Maru. The big man is beginning to stir. "Best we talk elsewhere." She nods, but doesn't move. When Brama touches her shoulder, she nods a second time, and the two of them leave together.

I n the southwestern quarter of Sharakhai, not so far
from the banks of the Haddah, lies the Temple of
Nalamae. Save for a few special nights of the year, the
broken temple lies empty. Disused. Forgotten and
mostly shunned by the citizens of Sharakhai. And yet
no one would dare tear it down, not even the Kings.
One might ignore the gods of the desert without fear
of retribution, but attempting to erase their memory
entirely would be like waving a ribbon before a black
laugher and daring it to charge.

The temple is where Brama decides to take Jax. It's
also the very place I was taken, captured, and caught
within the falcon's egg sapphire Brama now wears
around his neck. Perhaps Brama wishes to taunt me
by coming here. If that's the case, he has succeeded,
for this is also the place where my most loyal servant,
Kadir, died, and I feel a growing sadness and anger.
The lives of mortals may be fleeting, but Kadir's blazed
higher and brighter than the dim candles of most souls
in Sharakhai.

Brama motions Jax to walk ahead of him into the
temple. He slows, watching the way behind, wary
of Kymbril's gang, wary of the assassin. No one is
following, however, and the two of them head into
the nave, where the temple's grand, broken dome arcs

high above them. Rubble and stone and dust lay all about. The mosaics here depict life in the earliest days of Sharakhai: the river, the mount where the Kings' palaces were built, the small settlement that grew into the sprawling metropolis that eventually swallowed the open land around this temple.

The colors around Jax are bright, especially as she walks in shadow. They're more vivid than they've ever been. Surely she will be the one to release me from my prison. Or deliver me to the one who will. She's restless. I can feel it inside her: the worry over her pursuers, the desire to return to her homeland, the sad and growing realization that she no longer can.

She reaches the center of the open space and stares up at the jagged gap where the dome had been sundered, a remnant of Goezhen's presence here nearly two centuries ago. "My mother and father were murdered nearly one year ago in a temple not so different from this one." Her voice is weak, subdued. "It honored the gods of the mountains, among them Nehiran and Urajaxan, after whom Nehir and I were named. It did little to save my parents, but Nehir still thought it a fortuitous sign that the two of us were able to escape. I believed him then—that our patron gods were watching over us—but I can see now it was only my fear speaking to me, words of hope whispered to a petrified girl." She laughs a bitter laugh and stoops to pick up a stone. She turns it absently in her hand, continues to walk, taking in the grandness of this ruined place. "How foolish we were. The gods care nothing for our struggles. We soon found out from those still loyal to our family that all had been arranged beforehand. After my parents were murdered, our land was delivered to my father's rival in exchange for a ruby mine our own lord had had his eye on for decades. We hoped to rally support to restore the power of our house, but when our few allies were also killed, we knew the time was upon us to flee." She spins, flinging her arms wide like a mummer performing a play; the lights surrounding her dance along with her. "We came here to Sharakhai, but even this city wasn't far enough. The lords who conspired to kill my parents will never allow Nehir and me to live. We are the final two who have a rightful claim to our barony. They cannot take the chance that we'll reach our king and present our case. That's why the assassins follow us, even here. That's why they won't stop until we're dead."

Brama sits on a large piece of rubble. He speaks, keeping an eye on the temple's entrances. "Your troubles… Is that why Nehir took to smoking lotus?"

Without pulling her gaze from the mosaics, she nods. "That's when he started selling as well. My father knew several smugglers of the black, and allowed them to pass through our lands—with a tax, of course. Nehir was being groomed to take on more responsibility from my father, and had learned their names. He made contact with them immediately after reaching Sharakhai, thinking he'd rebuild our wealth—some small amount of it, in any case, enough to return to Malasan to hire swords and spears to aid his cause. One hundred good soldiers, he told me. One hundred is all we need. If we get that many, a thousand more will rally to our side."

"And would they?"

Jax laughs. "No. Our people did not hate our father, but neither did they love him. And with both dukes standing united, our cause is lost. Had we ten thousand, we would still fall beneath their combined might."

"So what will you do? Kymbril won't let this stand. He wants Nehir's head, too." He leaves unsaid that the drug lord likely wants Jax dead as well; he can see in her eyes she already knows.

"I'll book passage on a caravan ship."

"To where?"

She shrugs. "Kundhun. From there we'll continue

on, far enough that they'll stop chasing us."

"That may work," Brama says into the cool breeze, "but I think it likely you'll need to leave your brother behind."

"I know." She scrapes the dirt from under her fingernails. "He won't want to go, but I have to convince him. He doesn't know this city, and he has yet to accept the fact that we'll never return home to Malasan."

Disappointment emanates from Brama like heat from a hearth. He's only just met Jax, but there's something about her that entrances him. His old self might already have started to woo her, to get her by his side, to cajole her into bed—his old self would have tried harder precisely because she would soon be leaving the city—but this Brama, the changed Brama, simply wants a friend. I can feel the desire in him mixing imperfectly with the acceptance that her departure is necessary.

"Finding passage on a caravan won't be difficult," he says, "nor would it be expensive if you're willing to work the ship. But buying their silence. That will be expensive. Now that we've beaten Maru senseless, Kymbril isn't going to let this go, and I doubt your Dukes will either."

She fixes her gaze on Brama at last. "That's why I

need you. I don't know which caravan masters to trust."

"Do you have money?"

"Yes."

"How much?"

"Enough."

Brama shakes his head. "I have to know what I'm dealing with. The more you can spend, the safer a caravan master I can find for you. Skimping here might cost you your life."

I would laugh if I had form. She's staring into Brama's eyes, trying to weigh just how far she can trust him, but she's in too deep to be questioning such things. Still, Brama remains silent, waiting patiently as she takes in the scars on his face, on his hands. "Who did this to you?"

"A vile creature."

"Did you kill it?"

"No, but there are days when I wish I had."

The power within her has been muted until this moment. Now it ignites, and I can see some of the upbringing of a Malasani noble. "There are days when I tell myself I should return to Malasan and avenge the death of my parents. But then I remember how narrowly we escaped, how close we've come to death since then." She reaches down and pulls up one trouser leg. She rolls down her woolen sock all the way to the ankle, exposing three bracelets. Immediately Brama's old instincts for assessing the value of goods return to him. Two of the bracelets are gold. They're beautifully made though simple in design. Each would fetch a handsome price, but nothing like what she'd need to buy discrete, long-distance passage for two aboard a caravan ship. The third, however, is made of white gold, and is strung with small rubies and diamonds. "This is the last of what I smuggled away from Malasan, and the last of what I've managed to keep hidden from Nehir." Of the three, she unclasps the one with the rubies and diamonds and hands it to Brama. "Will it be enough?"

"More than enough. It will ensure you get help to go wherever you wish and help when you arrive as well. But first we need to convince Nehir."

The sounds of the city are distant and muted, but now Brama hears the sound of scraping, the subtle shift of leather on sand-dusted stone. Brama knows immediately it comes from somewhere in the temple. He turns toward it, waits, holding up a hand up to Jax for silence. He listens for the span of two breaths, then rushes silently toward her. Together they move toward the rear of the temple.

Brama whispers to her, "Where is your brother

now?"

She hesitates, her eyes fearful as she glances over her shoulder for their pursuer. "In a room above the Dancing Mule."

Brama nods. "I'll find you there." Then he points her toward the opposite side of the stone-walled courtyard. Beyond lay the Haddah, and a dozen paths of escape for Jax if she's fast enough. Brama waits for her to leave and slips behind a tall marble statue of a woman cradling a lamb. From behind it he watches the shadowed doorways of the temple. I wish to reach out, to find the man who's following him wherever he may hide, but Brama denies me.

Across the courtyard, a stone balustrade divides a patio from the sandy yard beyond. At the yard's far end stands a grove of decorative trees, all nearly barren of leaves. It is there that Brama sees shadows shifting. A split second too late, he jerks back behind the statue. A dark line slices the air. A crack breaks the stillness as the leg of the statue is chipped by the streaking arrow. Brama feels a sharp pain along the outside of his knee. Sucking air through gritted teeth, he examines the wound.

But then, before I know what's happening, he's pulled Maru's knife and is sprinting toward the trees.

I plead with him to take the protection I can offer, but he refuses; his decision to help Nehir is an embarrassing moment of weakness for him. He can see the assassin clearly now—his bow is drawn, the string to his ear—but Brama doesn't flinch.

He's going to die, I realize. He's moving with intent and pure abandon and little else. He's touching that place where he hid while I tortured him. It is a place of fear and rage and dwindling hope. I never thought to find a place of commonality with a mortal, but I too was tortured. I too found a place like this. It makes me feel no sympathy for Brama—what is he but a tool I will use to win back my freedom?—but there, in that hidden place so tightly tied to us both, I realize I can feel him more strongly than at any time except when he used me to lift Nehir's addiction.

I allow some of myself to filter through Brama, adding my rage to his. As the arrow is released, our combined power pours forth. The arrow flies, turns black as it nears us. The arrow's point digs into Brama's leather vest, bites his scar-riddled skin, but goes no further as the shaft of the arrow sprays outward from the point of impact in a brilliant fan of smoke and glowing red embers.

The assassin's eyes go wide. He pauses for a moment, his indecision clear, and then he drops his bow, sprints toward the temple wall behind him, leaps against it, and clings to a lattice of dried vines. Then he clambers over the top. Brama tries to follow, sprinting to the wall, but the wound along his knee flares; the puncture wound in his chest burns as he pulls himself up along the vines. By the time he drops to the city street on the other side, the assassin is gone. It is in this moment, while Brama is staring along the empty street, that I wonder if Brama saw what I saw. I pray to Goezhen he hasn't, for as the assassin leapt over the wall, a trace of light trailed in his wake, there and gone in a moment, a thing I'd not thought to see, but now that I have it's making me reconsider all the events that had led us to this point.

Across the street, on the sill of an open window, sits a massive copper kettle. Brama walks toward it, pulling the necklace over his head as he goes. Gripping the leather cord tightly in one hand, he stares into the ruddy reflection of his face that grows the nearer he comes to it. The reflection transforms, becomes the distorted face of an ehrekh.

"How did you do it?" Brama asks.

"I don't know what you mean."

"You know precisely what I mean. How did you

ignite the arrow without my leave?"

"You willed it."

"That's a bloody lie." His hand is gripped so tightly my prison, the sapphire, shakes. "You worked through me of your own free will."

I pause, knowing that the wrong words here could make Brama do something rash. I'm consoled by the realization that he didn't notice the light trailing the assassin, or perhaps he did and thought it some vestige of the power I unleashed. "You cannot expect the two of us to remain close for as long as we have without some effect. What I did, I did to protect you."

"What you did, you did to protect you." He lifts the necklace, stares at its cloudy facets. "You cannot do it again. I forbid it."

"You are the master who holds the chains," I say to him, an ancient proverb, one that was once used bitterly by the powerless but in recent centuries has come to mean simple deference. He can sense the way I'm chafing at my imprisonment, but I continue. "He may have heard Jax. He may be on the way to the tavern now."

Brama stares uncertainly into the kettle, but when an elderly woman shuffles toward the window from inside, he slips the necklace back around his head and sprints headlong for the Haddah and the bridges that span it, his worry for Jax growing with each long stride he takes.

Brama reaches the Drunken Mule at a run. He takes the stairs at the back of the old, misshapen tavern to the balcony that leads to four rooms situated above the common room. Brama doesn't know which one is Jax's, but the door to the second room is open. He paces toward it, body tensed, and finds Jax standing just inside. She's holding something in her hand. As Brama comes closer, he sees she's holding a severed finger in a blood-stained kerchief.

"Kymbril," Brama says.

Jax nods. Her hands are shaking.

Brama takes it from her and sees a small wooden chit, half hidden by Nehir's severed digit. There's a symbol on it—Kymbril's own—a coiled viper. "It's a message."

"I know what it is!" Her eyes are saucers. She's shaking so badly her lips are trembling. "I'm going to go there. I'm going to save him."

"You don't understand." He holds up the chit, then

wraps the finger in the kerchief and sets it on a simple ironwork table near the door. "This is a marker for those who buy large amounts of black lotus or white-fire or what have you. They get it after bringing the money to men like Maru, at which point they take it to another location to pick up their purchase. Kymbril wants you, but he also wants Nehir's stash."

She looks ready to argue, but then her resolve hardens and she holds out her hand. "Give me the bracelet."

She means the one she gave him at the temple, the one bright with diamonds and rubies. "You can't buy him off, Jax. Not anymore. He wants both of you dead."

She flicks her fingers. "Give it to me! It's mine!"

"It won't work."

Her face screws up in anger, and she begins pummeling him with her balled-up fists, striking him inexpertly around the shoulders and chest. Brama doesn't try to stop her. He takes it all, her swings thudding into his chest, slapping against his face. Eventually she stops and simply holds herself. "I can't let him go."

"You don't have to," Brama says as he steps in and takes her into his arms. Surprisingly, she allows it, even softening as he continues to hold her. Brama speaks softly and strokes her hair, "Here's what we're going to do."

In the heart of the Knot lies Kymbril's manor, where he runs his operations. It stands drunkenly with its neighbors at the end of a cul-de-sac. Lying low as he is on the roof of the building next to Kymbril's, Brama can see the full length of the street. He's watching for Kymbril's spotters, those who look for danger and call it out before it lands on his very doorstep. There are two boys sitting at the mouth of an alley halfway down the street. Seeing them crouched, preoccupied with a game of sticks, Brama picks up the fragrant calfskin sack by his side and moves smooth and low to the nearby roof of Kymbril's building. With the buildings butting up against one another, it's as simple as dropping a few feet down over the lip of the building. Once there, he sets the sack down, removes his necklace, and ties a length of string to the leather cord. Moving to the very front of Kymbril's building, he feeds the string out, lowering the necklace until the sapphire is suspended in the corner of the topmost window below.

After securing the string to a nail, he lies flat and closes his eyes. Like the coming of dawn shedding light over a dangerous landscape, a vision of the room brightens in Brama's mind. The drapes Brama spotted earlier while surveilling the building mask the sapphire's presence, but the cloth's material is thin enough that he can see the room within. Kymbril is there, leaning deeply into a couch along the far wall, staring through the window where the sapphire now hangs. Brama's heart skips, but he realizes Kymbril's eyes are closed. He's asleep, his breath coming long and slow. He looks as though he fell onto the couch the night before and has yet to wake up.

On the roof, Brama opens his eyes and blinks. He stares at the blue sky, breathing deeply and yawning like a jackal to help clear the dizziness from his mind and body. The effects of the gem are disorienting, but he's handling it well enough. Before Brama left for Kymbril's manor, I offered more of my power to him—much more, in fact—but he's still wary of me, enough that this facile spell is the one small concession to Jax's desperate need he allowed.

He closes his eyes again and studies the room, memorizing it. With Kymbril so vulnerable, he considers slipping in through the window and driving a knife into his chest, but it would be too risky. He doesn't know where Nehir is being kept, and he promised Jax he would do everything he could to see her brother safe, so he resolves to continue as planned.

I muse at how quickly mortals can fall for another soul; I suppose we're not so different in this respect.

Soon, Jax appears at the far end of the street. She walks with a tightness, hands bunched at her sides. Even far away it's easy to see how frightened she looks. A good amount of it is real, to be sure, but she's playing her part well. They want Kymbril to see her as a scared little doe, ready to bolt at a sharp sound or sudden movement. A boy struts out to meet her, dust kicking up behind him into the hot air. He holds his hand out and says something, not quite loud enough for Brama to hear, but Jax shakes her head, demanding she be allowed to see her brother.

The boy shouts at her, "You were to have brought it here," angry that she doesn't have Nehir's stash.

"Bring her," calls a voice from the base of Kymbril's manor.

Maru. Part of Brama regrets not drawing his knife across Maru's throat in the tenement, but if it wasn't Maru it would be someone else. It's a simple truth in the Shallows: finding oneself with a shortage of those willing to do dark work for a bit of coin only means you haven't looked hard enough.

As the boy leads Jax into Kymbril's manor, Brama waits, hoping he hasn't miscalculated. It wouldn't be the worst thing if Kymbril meets her below, but he's counting on Jax being brought to Kymbril's private offices, where it will be easier to make their escape.

Brama takes up the bulky sack, which smells strongly of fermented lotus, and crawls to the trap door leading down into the building. He sets the sack down, closes his eyes, and waits breathlessly as the sounds of the city play around him. The clatter of hooves in the distance, the rattle of wheels. The sound of children playing, a man coughing so heavily and wetly Brama wonders if he already stands on the threshold of the farther fields. Maru's voice calls up the stairs, and Kymbril wakes. The big man shakes his head, uses the heel of his hands to clear the sleep from his eyes, then opens the door to the room. Jax, guided by Maru, takes the last run of stairs to the topmost level and steps inside the room, where Maru pulls her to a stop.

Kymbril makes a show of looking her up and down. "Takes a lot of nerve, coming here empty-handed."

"You'll get the lotus," Jax replies nervously, "but only after I see my brother."

"You think you can come here, to my house, and start making demands?"

66

"You want our stash and you want us gone," Jax says evenly. "All I'm asking is to make sure he's unharmed."

Kymbril laughs at that. "Other than his finger, you mean."

Jax stares back defiantly. "I will see my brother. Only then will you see your reek."

"I don't need your reek, girl."

"We have a lot of it, Kymbril."

The statement sits between them like a jewel for the taking. Kymbril considers a moment, then nods to Maru, who leaves and heads downstairs. He returns a short while later with Nehir, a black bag over his head, in tow. Maru removes the bag to reveal a face that is bruised and bloodied. He cradles his right hand, tightly wrapped in a bloody bandage, to his chest. The resignation in Nehir's face is plain to see, as if he's known for months that it would come to this, and now that it has there's precious little to do but accept it.

Jax reaches up and brushes his hair, tenderly, slowly. She's positioned herself as Brama instructed so that neither Maru nor Kymbril can see the words written on her wrist. To his credit, Nehir's expression hardly changes. He becomes more calm, a tell in and of itself, but the gods of his homeland are watching over him, for neither Kymbril nor Maru seem to notice.

"Enough." Kymbril steps between the two of them and turns to face Jax. "Where's the ruddy stash?"

She puts her fingers to her lips and whistles. On cue, Brama stands and stomps on the trap door on the roof. Through the crystal eye he sees Kymbril and Maru staring up toward the ladder against the wall and the trap door it leads to.

"What's this?" Kymbril growls.

"Your stash," Jax says.

Kymbril raises a thumb at Maru, and Maru climbs the ladder to the trapdoor and pushes it open. On the roof, Brama opens his eyes, replacing the sapphire's perspective with his own, and makes his way down the ladder. He tosses the heavy sack at Kymbril's feet. Kymbril stares at it, then at him. Then he smiles wide, looking like a little boy who's just been served his favorite meal from his memma. Kneeling, Kymbril opens the sack and takes a good whiff of the pile of fermented black lotus petals. "I'll give it to you, Brama," Kymbril says. "You almost had me convinced you were innocent in all this." He stands and steps closer to Brama, pulls his shirt out and looks down his bare chest. "Where's that necklace of yours?"

Brama's only reply is to unclasp two of Jax's bracelets, the simpler ones, from around his wrist. He flips them in the air to Kymbril, who catches them with ease and stares, a quizzical look on his rough-and-tumble face. "What's this?"

"Enough, along with the reek, to let them leave the city unharmed. They'll be no further trouble to you, Kymbril. That I promise. If they come back, I'll take the knife to them myself."

"Ah, but we know what your promises mean."

"What Nehir did was more than foolish," Brama continues. "You've made that clear. But he was only trying to raise money to head home and avenge the deaths of his parents. A fool's dream. We can all see that now. Can't we, Nehir?"

Nehir stares at everyone in turn. Wearily, he nods to Kymbril.

Brama goes on, "They've both given up, Kymbril. They're leaving the city, far enough away that Sharakhai and their troubles in Malasan will be but a memory."

Kymbril shrugs. "You know how this city works, boy. Always mongrel dogs nipping at your heels. My soldiers see I let these two go, what will they think? Or worse, my enemies?"

Brama considers this. "What if you and I could come to some sort of arrangement? What if I remained in your employ and helped heal those most addicted to the reek?" Kymbril and Maru exchange a look. It's clear that Nehir confessed what Brama had done for him, but surely the two men had scoffed at the notion. Brama speaks quickly before either man can protest. "What I did with Nehir I can do again. I'll do so whenever you ask."

"Even if you could, how would that help me?"

"Because when your wealthiest patrons die, you lose a reliable source of income, but what if the lotus's call was removed from them before that happened?"

"I'd lose them."

"Some perhaps, but certainly not all. And if you sensed that they were falling too far, you could force them to pay coin for it. You'd win either way, Kymbril, and fewer would die."

Brama's words take me aback. This is either something Brama just thought of or purposely hid from me. Either way, in all our days together, I've never felt this from him—a spark amidst the terrible darkness surrounding him—and I wonder what will come of it.

Kymbril, however, merely frowns. "I'll admit I'm intrigued, boy. Yesterday it might've been enough to call things square. Yesterday, I was in a giving mood. But I made another deal this morning. Can't go back on it now."

Fresh footsteps can be heard from below. Brama tenses as a dark form ascends the stairs. Jax and Nehir look at each other anxiously. This is something neither he nor Jax nor I had considered.

The man is one they all recognize: the assassin. What has me transfixed, more than his sudden appearance, are the lights that dance around him. They're dazzling, nearly blinding. And I realize Jax has become as dull as an old copper coin. It's true, then. Jax's role has always been to lead me to the assassin.

He steps into the room and looks at Nehir and Jax. Apparently satisfied, he tosses a bag to Kymbril. It clinks as Kymbril snatches it from the air. Kymbril opens the bag and inspects the contents. "May your daughters find husbands and your sons wives," he says with a wide grin, then shoves Jax toward the door.

"No!" Nehir shouts, and leaps into Jax's path.

Brama is already on the move. He stomps hard on Maru's foot, twists and elbows him in the jaw. Maru reels, and Brama sends him flying backward, through the doorway and toward the stair rails. Before Kymbril can react, Brama brings his heel down sharply onto the sack. The muffled sound of a bladder bursting emanates from the sack. A sizzling follows. Then green smoke rises from the bag.

Brama dives toward the corner of the room to avoid Kymbril's grasp.

"Away, Nehir!" Jax shouts as she too runs for the far corner of the room.

But it's too late. The assassin stabs Nehir in the belly with a sharp thrust of his knife. Nehir stumbles, tries to crawl away.

When a high-pitched whistling sound comes from the bag, Brama clamps his eyes shut, and the center of the room transforms into a burst of white light. On and on it goes, the shrieking sound, the bright light so strong it's all Brama can do to keep it out. The skin along his left side burns hot, and he worries that the concoction he'd bought from the alchemyst with Jax's third bracelet was too much, that they'd all go up in flames, but he no sooner has this thought than the light and sound and heat all subside. Soon the only sounds are the moaning of men and a sizzling like meat over an open fire. Brama realizes he's on the floor, fingers grasping for purchase. He turns himself over, sees Jax standing in the corner, eyes dazed and blinking, yawning as she shakes her head.

Kymbril is not far from her, unconscious. The front of his clothes are charred; the legs of his trousers still smoke.

Near the open door, where the sack of black lotus once was, a hole is burned clear through the flooring and the timbers to the room below. Blue-green fire licks around the hole and up the door frame, where the flames transition to something more mundane: an orange the color of turning leaves. Nehir lies in the hall, grasping his gut, pulling at the banister in a vain attempt at regaining his feet. Past him runs Maru, back into the room with his knife drawn.

Brama stands to meet him. He takes one step forward, pretending to charge, but when Maru lowers his shoulder, preparing for it, Brama drops onto his back, lifts his legs, and catches Maru's gut with both feet. Maru swings his knife wildly at Brama, slicing his arm, but Brama uses Maru's momentum against him. With an almighty thrust of his legs, he launches Maru into the air and through the window behind him. As Maru grasps for the window frame, his knife tumbles into the corner. A moment later a thud and a groan come as Maru lands on the ground outside.

Brama rolls over one shoulder and takes up Maru's knife as Kymbril, mouth gaping, makes it to one knee.

The assassin, meanwhile, stands in the doorway, his left arm burned and blistered. The lights swirl around him, and I am transfixed. I can do little, but I reach out to him. With all my will I beckon him, I force him to notice the glint in window. I whisper but one small memory: an arrow that bursts into flame as it strikes his enemy's chest.

As Brama moves to engage Kymbril, the assassin moves to the window. He reaches out and grasps the necklace. With a downward tug, he snaps the string holding it in place. By Goezhen's sweet kiss, what we might do together, he and I. For a time, he will be the one in control, I have no doubt, but with someone like him holding the necklace—I can already feel his eagerness, his ambition—it won't be long before I am the master of my fate once more. Perhaps then we'll return to Malasan. Perhaps I'll allow him to accept commissions from his lords. I could do with a bit of murder to quench the fire that's been building within me. Or perhaps I'll move on, toss the assassin aside and take the form of one of his lords. It's been too long since I've been to Malasan in any case. The last time I was there it wasn't even called Malasan.

Brama and Jax are wrestling with Kymbril. Kymbril tries gouging Brama's eyes, but Jax raises a knife high overhead and plunges it into Kymbril's neck. Blood sprays over her, over Brama. Kymbril thrashes as the two of them stand and back away. Then the big man with the mismatched eyes goes still, his hands grasping empty air. Finally his body goes still, and Brama and Jax turn to the assassin. Nehir is there as well, on his feet, hands pressed against his stomach, his face white as salt. Together, the three of them hem the assassin in.

Brama eyes the sapphire in the assassin's hand, but he knows something has changed. He can feel it. A distancing from me, which, even though he'd come to resent it, leaves an empty space inside him.

"You don't have to do this," Brama says.

The words are for me, not the assassin, but the assassin still responds. "All of this is necessary." He grips the sapphire tight. Wills me to burn them all as I burned the arrow.

But there's something about Brama that gives me pause. I haven't seen him through another's eyes in years, and when last I had he was dull, almost lifeless. Back then, I hardly spent a moment on him, blinded as I was by my obsession with the White Wolf.

But now…

There are lights, but they are dark and difficult to see. They remind me of my lord Goezhen. Will Brama be touched by the God of Demons? Will he one day stand before the lord who made me? It is something

I've given up on ever happening again, thinking my god abandoned me. But if it might be so, what a fool I'd be to pass it up. And yet it isn't up to me. Not me alone, in any case.

Nearby, the green, alchemycal fire is dead, and a mundane fire of flickering orange burns in its place. The smoke is growing, but no one pays attention to it. The assassin has opened his mind to me, enough that I can take his body from him for a time. "If I remain," I say with the assassin's voice, "will you allow me to help you?"

"What's happening?" Nehir asks, leaning against the wall. As he slides to the floor, his confused gaze flits between Brama and the assassin. Jax rushes to his side, every bit as confused as her brother, but Brama understands all too well who voiced that question.

"I will not kill for you," he says.

"You hold the reins, Brama. I only wish to help."

Brama stares, clenching his teeth.

"Brama—" Jax begins, but when Brama holds his hand up, she goes silent. Brama looks the assassin in the eye, and I know his answer before he gives it.

"Very well," he says.

And I nod back to him.

With a voice given to me by the God of Chaos

himself, I whisper to the assassin's mind. I tell him a story, of how he came to Sharakhai, how he found Jax and Nehir, how he made a deal with a local drug lord to secure them. I tell him how he slit both their throats, completing his lords' mission here in the desert. I breathe into him the satisfaction the deed gave him, and he swells from it.

As I knew it would, the urge to return to Malasan after long months spent tracking his quarry here to the slums of Sharakhai is born inside him. Slipping his knife into its sheath, he drops the crystal and walks through the smoke, beyond the flames, and down the stairs.

When he is gone, Brama walks to the where the necklace fell. He picks it up and slips it around his neck.

One week later, Jax stands at the door to the room that was once Kymbril's bedroom. "There's a man downstairs asking to see the Tattered Prince. He's the cousin of the girl you put right yesterday."

"How bad is he?"

"Bad," Jax replies.

Brama stands from the chair he'd been sitting in and begins to stretch. "Tell him I'll speak with him."

Jax stares. "You can't mean to heal him now."

"I do, if he can convince me of his earnestness."

He heads for the pair of beds that sit along the far side of the room. Brama will lie in one, the lotus addict the other, and then he and I will work together to lift the addiction and place it on Brama so that the man might be freed.

"But you've only just recovered."

"Maybe, but I am recovered. Send him up."

"Gods," Jax says under her breath. She stares at Brama as if he were some unanswerable riddle. "You'll kill yourself if you keep going."

"Perhaps. But I'm giving people new chances at life."

He's used that term once or twice before, and it has struck Jax hard each time. Nehir died the night of the fight with Kymbril from the wound to his gut. They buried him in the sand the following morning. When it was done, Brama asked Jax what she planned to do.

"I don't know," she said, staring out at the eastern horizon, toward Malasan. "Part of me wishes to return to my home. Part of me wishes to leave and go to Kundhun as I'd planned." She turned to Brama then.

"And part of me would stay."

It was an offer, a plea, as clear as she could make it just then.

Brama smiled, a bit of the scoundrel returning to him. "Stay for a day. Stay for a week. I'll show you parts of the city you'd never find on your own."

As she stared into his eyes, a genuine smile crossed her lips. "I'd like that."

But she hadn't counted on Brama following through on his offer to Kymbril. The very next day, he healed two of the worst addicts who'd wound up in the lowest floor of Kymbril's manor, freeing them from the prison the lotus had built around them.

In the manor, Jax strides to Brama's side and takes his hand. "Promise me you'll be careful?" She leans in and kisses him, pulling away as quickly as she'd come. "We have sights to see, you and I."

I feel him brighten from within, and a smile most genuine spreads across his face. "I will be."

The look they share is precious, one of the most beautiful things I've seen in Sharakhai, a tattered prince and a young, foreign noble. And then Jax leaves the room to lead the suffering man up.

When she's gone, Brama moves to a beaten brass mirror hung against the wall. "Are you ready?"

"Of course, my master."

"I asked you not to call me that."

In the mirror, my visage smiles. "You don't have to suffer like this, you know. There are a thousand things and a thousand more we could do together. You and I and the girl."

"To live is to suffer," Brama replies. "I merely wish to do something virtuous with my life for once."

I consider this, wondering where the dark lights I'd seen will take him. Where they will take me.

"Very well," I say. "I'm ready."

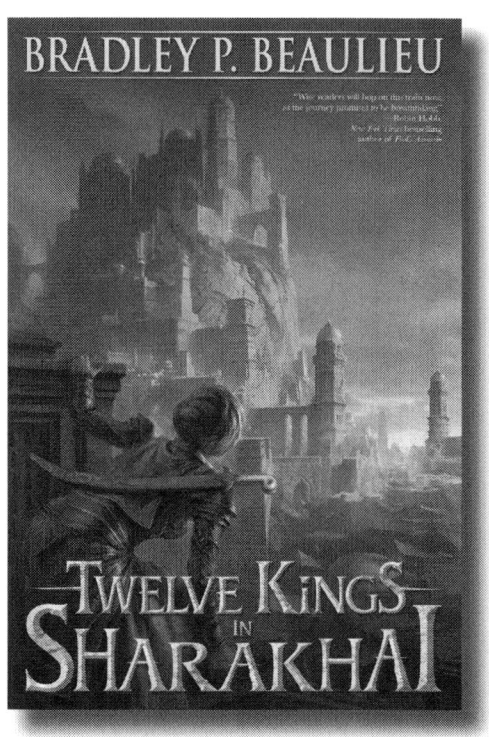

Continue the adventure in *Twelve Kings in Shara-khai*. A sample of the book's first chapter follows...

Chapter 1

In a small room beneath the largest of Sharakhai's fighting pits, Çeda sat on a wooden bench, tightening her fingerless gloves. The room was cool, even chill compared to the ever-present heat of the city. Painted ceramic tiles lined the walls. A mismatched jumble of wooden benches and shelves that had clearly seen decades of abuse made it feel well loved if not well cared for. Were Çeda any other dirt dog, she would have sat in one of the rooms on the far side of the pits, the ones that hosted dozens of men and women. But Çeda was given special dispensation, and had been since winning her first bout at the age of fourteen.

By the gods, five years already.

She tightened her hands into fists, enjoying the creak of the leather, the feel of the chain mail wrapped around the backs of her hands and knuckles. She checked the straps of her armor. Her greaves, her bracers, her heavy battle skirt. And finally her breastplate. All of them had once been dyed white—the color of a wolf's bared teeth—but now the armor was so well used that much of the leather's natural brown shone through. *Well and good*, Çeda thought. It felt used. Lived in. Kissed by battle. Exactly the way she liked it.

She picked up her bright steel helm and set it on her lap. She stared into the iron mask fixed across the front—a mask of a woman's face, cold and expressionless in the face of battle. Affixed to the top of the helm was a wolf's pelt, teeth bared, muzzle resting along the crown.

Echoing down the corridor came a voice that sounded old and hoary, a mountain come to life. "They're ready." It was Pelam.

Çeda glanced toward the arched doorway with the blood-red curtains strung across it. "Coming," she said, then returned her attention to the helm. She ran her fingers over the many nicks in the metal, over the mask's empty eyes—

Tulathan grant me foresight.

—stroked the rough fur of the wolf's pelt—

Thaash guide my sword.

—then pulled the helm over her braided black hair and strapped it tightly on.

As the weight of the armor settled over her, she parted the heavy curtains and hiked up the sloping tunnel into the heat of the noontime sun. The walls of the fighting pit towered around her, and above them, arranged in concentric circles, were the seats of the stadium. *It's going to be a good day for Osman.* Already there were several hundred waiting for the bout to begin.

Roughly half the spectators called the city of Sharakhai home; they knew the pits inside and out, knew the regular dirt dogs as well. The other half were visitors to the desert's amber jewel. They'd come to trade or find fortune in a city that offered greater opportunities than they'd had back home. It rankled that so many came here, to Çeda's home, and lived off it like fleas on a dog. Though she could hardly complain—

A boy in a teal kaftan pointed to Çeda wildly and called, "The White Wolf! The Wolf has come to fight!" and the crowd rose to their feet as one, craning their necks to see.

—the pits paid well enough.

A ragged cheer went up as she strode to the center of the pit and joined the circle of eleven other fighters. The money men in the stands began calling out odds for the White Wolf. She hadn't even been chosen to fight yet, so no one would know who her opponent would be, but many still flocked to be the first to wager their coin on her.

The other dirt dogs watched Çeda warily. Some knew her, but just like those in the audience, many of these fighters had come from distant kingdoms to try their hand against the best fighters in Sharakhai. Three women stood among those gathered—two well muscled, the third an absolute brute; she outweighed Çeda by three stone at least. The rest were men, some brawny, others lithe. One, however, was a tower of a man wearing a beaten leather breastplate and a conical helm with chain mail that lapped against his broad shoulders. Haluk. He stood a full head and a half taller than Çeda and stared at her like an ox readying a charge.

In response, Çeda strode toward him and pressed her thumb to an exposed edge on the back of her mailed gloves. She pressed hard enough to pierce skin, to draw blood. Haluk stared at her with confusion, then a wicked sort of glee, as Çeda stopped in front of him and pressed her bloody thumb to the center of his leather breastplate.

The crowd roared.

A new flurry of betting rose, while the rest of the audience jockeyed for position against the rim of the pit.

Çeda had just marked Haluk for her own, an ancient gesture that not all dirt dogs would respect, but these would, she reckoned. None of them would wish to fight Haluk, not in their first bout of the day. When Çeda turned away and returned to her place in the circle, all but ignoring Haluk, the naked anger on his face was slowly replaced with a look of cool assessment. *Good,* Çeda thought. He'd taken the bait and would surely choose her if she didn't choose him first.

When some but not all of the betting flurry had died down, Pelam stepped out from another darkened tunnel. The calls of betting rose to a tumult as the audience saw the first bout was ready to begin.

Pelam wore a jeweled vest, a brown kufi, and a red kaftan that was not only fashionable but fine, save for its hem, which was hopelessly dusty from its days sweeping the pit floors. In one of Pelam's skeletal hands he held a woven basket. As the fighters parted for him, he stepped to the rough center of their circle and flipped the basket lid open. After one last check around him to ensure all was ready, he shot his hand into basket's confines and lifted a horned viper as long as his lanky legs. The snake wriggled, swelling its hood and hissing, baring its fangs for all to see.

Pelam knew his business, but the snake made Çeda's hackles rise. Bites were rare but not unheard of, especially if one of the fighters was inexperienced and jumped when the snake drew near. Çeda knew enough to remain still, but foreigners didn't always follow Pelam's careful pre-bout instructions, and it wasn't always the person who jumped that the snakes chose to sink their fangs into.

As Pelam held the writhing snake, each of the fighters spread their legs wide until their sandaled or booted feet butted up against each other's. After a glance at each of the fighter's stances, and finding them proper, Pelam dropped the snake and stepped away.

It lay there, coiling itself tightly. The crowd shouted to the baked desert air, their voices rising to a fever pitch as each yelled the name of their chosen fighter. The fighters themselves remained silent. Oddly, the snake slithered toward Pelam for a moment, then seemed to think better of it and turned to glide over the sand to Çeda's left, then turned once more. And slithered straight through Haluk's legs.

Silence followed as a pit boy ran and snatched the viper by its tail, lowering it back into its basket as the snake spun like a woodworker's auger.

Pelam calmly awaited Haluk's choice.

The big man didn't hesitate. He made straight for Çeda and spat on the ground at her feet.

The crowd went wild. "The Oak of the Guard has chosen the White Wolf!"

Oak indeed. Haluk was a captain of the Silver Spears, and a tree of a man, but he was also a particularly *cruel* man, and it was time he learned a lesson.

Like jackals to a kill, the news drew spectators from neighboring pits. The stands were soon brimming with them.

As the rest of the fighters exited the pit, a dozen boys jogged out from the tunnels bearing wooden swords and shields and clubs. Çeda, as the challenged, would normally be allowed to choose weapons first, but she followed ancient custom; she had marked him, and thus *she* was the true challenger, not Haluk, so she bowed her head and waved to the weapons, granting first choice to Haluk. Most would have returned the honor, but Haluk merely grunted and chose one of the few weapons meant for both him and his opponent: the fetters.

The noise of the crowd rose until it was akin to thunder. Some laughed, others clapped. Some few even stared with naked worry at Çeda, who had clearly just been put at a severe disadvantage by Haluk's choice of weapon.

The fetters was a length of tough, braided leather. It was wrapped tightly around one of each fighter's wrists, keeping them in close proximity and ensuring a brawl.

While glaring intently at Haluk, Çeda held out her left hand, allowing Pelam to slip the end of the fetters around her wrist and tighten it. Pelam did the same to Haluk, then took a small brass gong and mallet from one of the boys.

The pit was cleared so that only Çeda, Haluk, and Pelam remained.

The doors to the tunnels closed.

And then, after a dramatic pause in which Pelam held the gong chest-high between the two fighters, he struck it and stepped away.

There was slack in the fetters, a situation Haluk would quickly attempt to remedy—his best hope, after all, lay in controlling Çeda's movement—but Çeda was ready for it. The moment Haluk lunged in to grab as much of the leather rope as he could, she darted forward, leaping and snapping a kick at his chin. When he retreated, Çeda charged, a move he clearly hadn't been expecting. His eyes widened as Çeda grabbed his clumsily raised arm and sent her fist crashing into his cheek.

She could feel the chain mail dig deep into the fighting gloves she wore, but it was worse for Haluk. He fell unceremoniously onto his rump, his conical helm flying off and thumping onto the dry dirt, kicking up dust as it went.

The crowd stood and howled its delight.

As his helm skidded well out of reach, Haluk rolled backward over his shoulder and came to a stand, so quickly that Çeda had no time to rush forward and end it.

Haluk raised one hand to his cheek, felt the blood from the patterned cuts the mail had left in his skin, then stared at his own hand with a look like he'd disappointed himself. And then his eyes went hard. He'd been pure bluster before, trying to intimidate Çeda, but now he was seething mad.

None so blind as a wrathful man, Çeda thought.

Haluk crouched warily and began wrapping the

fetters around his left wrist, over and over, slowly taking up the slack. Çeda retreated and pulled hard on the fetters, putting her entire body into it, making the leather scrape painfully along Haluk's arm. He ignored it and continued to wrap the restraints around his wrist. Çeda yanked on the fetters again, but he blunted the tactic with well-timed grips on the leather, the muscles along his arm rippling and bulging. He grinned, showing two rows of ragged teeth.

Çeda sent several kicks toward his thighs and knees, attacks meant more to test Haluk's reflexes than anything else. Haluk blocked them easily. She was just about to yank on the fetters again when he loosened his grip and rushed her. Çeda stumbled, pretending to lose her balance, and when Haluk came close she dove to her right and swept a leg across his ankles.

He fell in a heap, the breath whooshing from his lungs.

He grabbed for Çeda and managed to snag her ankle, but one swift kick from Çeda's free heel and she was up and dancing away while Haluk rose slowly to his feet.

The crowd howled again, many of the foreigners joining in, though they had no idea why. The Sharakani knew, though. They understood why bouts like this were so very rare.

Haluk hadn't been defeated in more than ten years of fighting in the pits. Çeda had rarely lost since her first bout, and she'd lost none in the past three years. Everyone knew how widely the story of this bout would be told, especially if Çeda took him in so cleanly a fashion. Few would dare utter the tale within Haluk's hearing, but the entire city would be alive with it by the end of the day.

And Haluk knew it. He stared into Çeda's eyes with an intensity that reeked of desperation. He would not be so easy to take again.

As the two of them squared off once more, the crowd went completely and eerily silent. The only sound was of Haluk's ragged breathing and Çeda's strong but controlled breaths from within the confines of her helm.

Haluk took one tentative step forward. Çeda stepped away, snatching up some of the slack in the fetters as she went. Haluk did the same until they both held a quarter of the length in reserve, leaving them a scant few strides from one another.

Haluk took two measured steps toward her. He was trying to close the distance, but he was no longer reckless. He was cautious, as a man who'd become a captain of Sharakhai's guard *should* be.

Çeda kicked at his legs again, connecting but doing little damage. That wasn't the point, though. She had to keep him on his guard until she was ready to move in. She snapped another kick and retreated, but she could only go so far. Haluk had drawn up more of the fetters, so Çeda released some of hers. Haluk strode forward, taking up more of the braided rope. Which forced Çeda to release more. Until she had none left.

He drew sharply on it, keeping his center low, his balance steady, and Çeda was drawn forward until she was just out of his striking range.

The crowd began to stamp their feet, the sound of it reverberating in the pit, but otherwise they were silent, rapt.

Haluk pulled again, harder now that they were so close. And that's when Çeda moved.

Using the tension on the fetters to pull herself forward, she launched herself with a leap, straight into his body. In his surprise, Haluk grasped for her neck, but she slipped her forearms inside his and grabbed two fistfuls of his lanky brown hair. She wrapped her legs around his waist, twisted them around his thighs, and locked her feet around his knees, hoping to trip him up and end this once and for all.

He didn't fall, however. He was too big. Too strong. And he did exactly what she would have done. He rose up, preparing to slam her against the ground.

At the high point of his lift, she did the only thing she could: she clung hard to his neck and waist.

When they came down, they came down hard. Pain burst across Çeda's back and rump as Haluk's full weight bore down on her. Through her coughing and the ringing in her ears, she could hear him laughing. "Foolish move, girl."

He tried to lift away, but she'd locked her arms around his neck. Her legs hugged tightly to his waist. He was strong, but he had no leverage to break her grip. Again and again he tried to lift himself away from her to give himself room to punch, but each time he did, she began slipping her arms around his neck to cut off his blood. He would drop to prevent it, and then they were back, body to body, breath coming hard and fast, the very intimate duel continuing as each struggled for any small amount of leverage.

Once, when he lifted his head too far away, she crashed her forehead against his. The lip of her helm left a long cut against his skin. Blood seeped down his forehead, along his nose. It pattered against her steel mask, filling her nostrils with the smell of it.

Then, in a sudden and furious move, Haluk lifted, slipping a forearm across her throat, managing to pin her down.

Immediately the crowd was up, shouting, raging. But it all became little more than a keen ringing in Çeda's ears. She heard her own heart thrumming. Felt Haluk's arm tighten further.

It was a strong move, a *wise* move under the conditions, but he'd left himself open. She slipped her right hand down along his left arm, near his elbow, where she'd have the most leverage, and pushed. She let out a guttural cry while muscling his arm up, which had the effect of propelling herself down along his body, just enough to slip her head under his armpit and out of the lock.

He tried to slip his arm back under her neck, but before he could, she grabbed the buckles along the far edge of his breastplate and hauled herself away, and now she was halfway to his back. Exactly where she wanted to be.

She reached her left arm—the one tied to the fetters—up and over his head. The rope slipped neatly down along his face and across his neck. Immediately she tightened her grip and drew the fetters back.

Haluk knew what was happening—he tried to

throw her off, at least enough to get his fingers beneath the fetters—but her grip was too sure. Still, he was a bull of a man. She grunted while gritting her teeth and arching her back. Her arms strained like cording on a ship's sails.

She thought surely he would have pounded his hand against the ground by now, giving up the match, or fallen unconscious, but he hadn't. He still struggled for air, his breath coming out in a desperate hiss, his mouth frothing from it. And then finally, all at once, his body went slack.

Çeda didn't hear the strike of Pelam's gong, marking the end of the bout.

But the crowd she heard.

Their elation could no longer be contained. They stomped their feet. They shook their fists. "The Wolf has won! The Wolf has won!"

Ignoring them, Çeda pushed Haluk onto his back and straddled his chest. She unwrapped the fetters and saw the blood drain from him, casting his face in a strange, deathly pallor.

His eyes blinked open. He stared into Çeda's eyes with a look of confusion, then took in his surroundings as if he had no idea where he was. The roaring crowd and Çeda's masked face soon registered, though, and a look of deep and inexpressible anger stole over him.

Çeda leaned down until they were chest-to-chest and whispered into his ear. "The next time you take your hands to your daughter, Haluk Emet'ava"—she pressed the thumbnail of her right hand into his side, in the depression between his fourth and fifth ribs—"it will go much worse for you." She leaned closer still and whispered, "The next time, it will be a knife in the dark, not a beating in the light." She rose, her legs still straddling him, and stared down into his eyes. "Do you understand?"

Haluk blinked. He made no acknowledgement of her demand, but there was shame in his eyes, a shame that spoke the truth of his crimes better than words ever could.

Like a wedge driving ever further into a thick piece of wood, she pressed her thumb deeper. "I would hear your answer."

He grimaced against the discomfort, licked his lips and glanced to the cheering crowd. Then he nodded to her. "I understand."

Çeda nodded back, then stood and stepped away.

Pelam had watched this exchange with a glint in his eye that landed somewhere between curious and concerned, but he made no mention of it. He merely turned and presented Çeda to the crowd with a bow of his head and a flourish of his hand. As some howled and others collected their winnings, Çeda was surprised to see that Osman himself had come to watch—Osman, the owner of these pits, a retired pit fighter himself, the man she'd had to trick to earn her first bout.

How far we've come since then.

He stood with the crowd on the topmost row. He was one of the very few—along with Pelam—who knew her true identity. She had no idea how long he'd been watching, but surely he'd caught the end. She couldn't tell if he was pleased or not. Çeda gave an exaggerated nod to the crowd, but she and Osman both knew it was meant for him.

He nodded back, then tugged his ear, which meant he wished to speak.

To speak, and perhaps more.

Twelve Kings in Sharakhai is available wherever fine books are sold.

Twelve Kings in Sharakhai is the exciting new Arabian Nights-inspired epic fantasy from the critically acclaimed author of The Lays of Anuskaya.

Sharakhai, the great city of the desert, center of commerce and culture, has been ruled from time immemorial by twelve kings—cruel, ruthless, powerful, and immortal. With their army of Silver Spears, their elite company of Blade Maidens, and their holy defenders, the terrifying asirim, the Kings uphold their positions as undisputed, invincible lords of the desert. There is no hope of freedom for any under their rule.

Or so it seems, until Çeda, a brave young woman from the west end slums, defies the Kings' laws by going outside on the holy night of Beht Zha'ir. What she learns that night sets her on a path that winds through both the terrible truths of the Kings' mysterious history and the hidden riddles of her own heritage. Together, these secrets could finally break the iron grip of the Kings' power…if the nigh-omnipotent Kings don't find her first.

With Blood Upon the Sand, Book Two of The Song of the Shattered Sands...

Çeda, now a Blade Maiden in service to the kings of Sharakhai, trains as one of their elite warriors, gleaning secrets even as they send her on covert missions to further their rule. She knows the dark history of the asirim—that hundreds of years ago they were enslaved to the kings against their will—but when she bonds with them as a Maiden, chaining them to her, she feels their pain as if her own. They hunger for release, they demand it, but with the power of the gods compelling them, they find the yokes around their necks unbreakable.

When Çeda and Emre are drawn into a plot of the blood mage, Hamzakiir, they sail across the desert to learn the truth, and a devastating secret is revealed, one that may very well shatter the power of the hated kings. They plot quickly to take advantage of it, but it may all be undone if Çeda cannot learn to navigate the shifting tides of power in Sharakhai and control the growing anger of the asirim that threatens to overwhelm her.

A Veil of Spears, Book Three of The Song of the Shattered Sands...

The Night of Endless Swords was a bloody battle that saw the death of one of Sharakhai's immortal kings. When former pit fighter Çeda narrowly escapes the battle and flees into the desert, she takes with her the secrets she learned while posing as a Blade Maiden. Foremost among these is the revelation that the asirim, the kings' frightening immortal slaves, are in fact Çeda's own ancestors, survivors of the fabled thirteenth tribe.

Çeda returns to Sharakhai, hoping to break the chains of the enslaved asirim and save her people. She soon discovers that the once-unified front of the kings is crumbling. Feeling their power slipping away, the kings vie for control over the city and the desert beyond.

As Çeda works to free the asirim and rally them to the defense of the thirteenth tribe, the Kings of Sharakhai prepare for a grand clash that may decide the fate of all.

Of Sand and Malice Made, a Shattered Sands novel...

Çeda is the youngest pit fighter in the history of Sharakhai. She's made her name in the arena as the fearsome White Wolf. None but her closest friends and allies know her true identity. But this all changes when she crosses the path of Rümayesh, an ehrekh, a sadistic creature forged aeons ago by the god of chaos.

The ehrekh are desert dwellers, but for centuries Rümayesh has lurked in the dark corners of Sharakhai, combing the populace for jewels that might interest her. Çeda flees the ehrekh's attentions, but that only makes Rümayesh covet her even more. Rümayesh grows violent. She threatens to unmask Çeda as the White Wolf, but the danger grows infinitely worse when she turns her attention to Çeda's friends. Çeda is horrified. She's seen firsthand the suffering left in Rümayesh's wake.

As Çeda fights to protect the people dearest to her, Rümayesh comes closer to attaining her prize and the struggle becomes a battle for Çeda's very soul.

The critically acclaimed trilogy, The Lays of Anuskaya, is now available in an omnibus edition.

Among inhospitable and unforgiving seas stands Khalakovo, a mountainous archipelago of seven islands, its prominent eyrie stretching a thousand feet into the sky. Serviced by windships bearing goods and dignitaries, Khalakovo's eyrie stands at the crossroads of world trade. But all is not well in Khalakovo. Conflict has erupted between the ruling Landed, the indigenous Aramahn, and the fanatical Maharraht, and a wasting disease has grown rampant over the past decade. Now, Khalakovo is to play host to the Nine Dukes, a meeting which will weigh heavily upon Khalakovo's future.

When an elemental spirit attacks an incoming windship, Prince Nikandr, is tasked with finding the child prodigy believed to be behind the summoning. Can the Dukes, thirsty for revenge, be held at bay?

Can Khalakovo be saved? The elusive answer drifts upon the Winds of Khalakovo…

Find more adventures in other worlds with *Lest Our Passage Be Forgotten & Other Stories*...

With *The Winds of Khalakovo*, Bradley P. Beaulieu established himself as a talented new voice in epic fantasy. Now, with the release of his premiere short story collection, Beaulieu demonstrates his ability to weave tales that explore other worlds in ways that are at once bold, imaginative, and touching. *Lest Our Passage Be Forgotten & Other Stories* contains 17 stories that range from the epic to the heroic, some in print for the first time.

This story collection features two stories from the world of The Lays of Anuskaya. "To the Towers of Tulandan" is a prequel story that tells of Nasim's travels with Ashan before he met Nikandr Khalakovo. And "Prima" is a sequel that reveals what becomes of the three sisters of Vostroma. Also included in the collection is a never-before-published story from Beaulieu's Norse-inspired world of Bryndlholt.

Twelve Kings in Sharakhai marked the start of a bold new epic fantasy series for critically acclaimed author Bradley P. Beaulieu.

In the Stars I'll Find You & Other Tales of Futures Fantastic features Beaulieu's science fictional work, from exploring far-flung worlds to finding what it means to be human through artificial intelligence to the cost of dividing ourselves—or ourself—through the use of technology.

In this short story collection, you'll find eleven tales that explore our very human relationship with technology, some in print for the first time.

ABOUT THE AUTHOR

Bradley P. Beaulieu fell in love with fantasy from the moment he started reading *The Hobbit* in third grade. From that point on, though he tried reading many other things, fantasy became his touchstone. He always came back to it, and when he started to dabble in writing, fantasy—epic fantasy especially—was the type of story he most dearly wished to share.

Twelve Kings in Sharakhai, the first book in his latest series, The Song of the Shattered Sands, was named to over twenty "Best of the Year" lists when it was released in 2015. His critically acclaimed series, The Lays of Anuskaya, has recently been released in omnibus form.

Brad, who recently became a full-time writer, lives in Racine, Wisconsin with his wife and two children. Beyond writing, cooking has become an obsession. His favorite dishes are French, Italian, and Mexican/Southwestern, but he is also fascinated by the art of bread baking.

For more, please visit www.quillings.com.

Made in the USA
Columbia, SC
21 May 2018